BIRMINGHAM LIBRARIES
DISCARD

BLUE SKY FREEDOM

Gaby Halberstam lived in South Africa until the age of fifteen, when she and her family moved to Britain. She began writing stories at the age of five. Gaby studied English at university, and although she went on to qualify as a lawyer, she knew from the first day that she would rather be writing. She now lives in London with her husband and three children. Apart from her husband, she has no pets, although her daughter is constantly bombarding her with pleas for a dog. *Blue Sky Freedom* is her first novel.

Check out our interview with Gaby at the back if you'd like to find out more about her and about South Africa.

Gaby
Halberstam

BLUE SKY
FREEDOM

MACMILLAN CHILDREN'S BOOKS

First published 2008 by Macmillan Children's Books
a division of Macmillan Publishers Limited
20 New Wharf Road, London N1 9RR
Basingstoke and Oxford
www.panmacmillan.com

Associated companies throughout the world

ISBN 978-0-330-45051-5

Text copyright © Gabrielle Halberstam 2008

The right of Gabrielle Halberstam to be identified as the
author of this work has been asserted by her in accordance
with the Copyright, Designs and Patents Act 1988.

All rights reserved. No part of this publication may be
reproduced, stored in or introduced into a retrieval system, or
transmitted, in any form or by any means (electronic, mechanical,
photocopying, recording or otherwise), without the prior written
permission of the publisher. Any person who does any unauthorized
act in relation to this publication may be liable to criminal
prosecution and civil claims for damages.

1 3 5 7 9 8 6 4 2

A CIP catalogue record for this book is available from
the British Library.

Typeset by Intype Libra Limited
Printed and bound in Great Britain by Mackays of Chatham plc, Kent

This book is sold subject to the condition that it shall not,
by way of trade or otherwise, be lent, resold, hired out,
or otherwise circulated without the publisher's prior consent
in any form of binding or cover other than that in which
it is published and without a similar condition including this
condition being imposed on the subsequent purchaser.

Acknowledgements

Thank you to Lucy Juckes, my more-than-agent, for being so unfailingly warm and positive and patient, and thank you to the godmothers: Melanie Edge, Sharon Flockhart, Sophie McKenzie, Julie Mackenzie and Moira Young, who watched over and helped this book to grow.

Thank you also to Harriet Wilson and all the team at Macmillan for their support and attention to detail.

Without the encouragement of my husband (who persisted despite my often deeply dug-in heels), the enthusiasm of our children and my mother's detailed memories that helped to bring so much of my childhood back to me, this book would not have happened at all.

To my father

Part One

South Africa, January 1975

Chapter One

It was the first day back after the Christmas holidays; my satchel was so stuffed with books it was creaking. I closed our gate behind me. There were still shreds of mango-coloured clouds, and I could smell the leftover night smells of honeysuckle and damp earth. My favourite time of day. The sun hadn't yet burned away the dew and there were horizontal spiders' webs hanging like trampolines between the blades of grass.

I trudged along, hoping I'd arrive early enough to get the desk I wanted (near the front), and wondering if I'd ever make it into the tennis team. An old black woman was ahead of me. She had a cloth bundle on her head, and she was singing a hymn. The broken backs of her shoes slapped at her bare heels as she sauntered down the road.

There was a clatter and grind as an old car came up behind us. The woman turned. She put her hands up to the bundle and tried to run. I looked over my shoulder. An oily yellow jeep was roaring up the road. Why was she running? Just then the jeep speeded up. It tore past me. Pellets of loose tarmac sprayed my legs. Its hooter blared. It drew level with the woman. Then shrieked to a stop just in front of her. Two policemen leaped out, one of them really tall. Again she tried to run. They each grabbed one of her arms. The bundle fell to the ground. The tall policeman kicked it, and it flew into the air, spinning comically. It landed almost without a sound on the grass verge and split open.

'Hey!' I shouted. I'd never seen anything like that before.

The woman struggled to get free. She began to cry.

'Ach, shut up!' The other policeman gave her a shove. She hit her head against the side of the jeep.

'Show us your Pass!' the policeman shouted.

She wrestled one arm free and patted her sides, checking the pockets of her faded maid's uniform. Her hand fluttered down the front of her dress. Nothing. The tall policeman flung open the cage doors at the back of the jeep.

'Get in, you fat old Kaffir!'

The woman shouted something and pointed at the bundle. I darted forward to gather up her stuff and give it to her, but the other policeman put his arm out to stop me.

'Leave it! What are you? Some kind of Kaffir-lover?' he snarled.

4

I stopped where I was. I was panting, my heart banging against my ribs.

The woman shouted out again. This time the tall policeman slapped her across her face. As she cowered he pulled her by the collar and pushed her into the back of the jeep. She scrabbled a bit and her dress rode up. She was wearing long, dazzlingly white, old-lady bloomers. The lace around the legs was tattered.

I couldn't bear it. I had to do something. I leaped again for the broken bundle. Maybe I could get it to her before the jeep drove off. But the policeman who'd shouted at me before moved to block my way. He stood so close to me my breath misted up his brass buttons.

'Didn't you hear me the first time, *meisie*? Buzz off before we put you in there as well!'

My chest began to heave. I could hardly breathe. Sweat was trickling down my back.

Meanwhile, the cage doors had been locked shut and the tall policeman was behind the wheel with the engine running. The other policeman strode to the passenger side of the jeep, slammed the door shut after him and they tore off. The woman looked back at me through the grid of the cage.

I stood where I was for a moment. I felt shaky. The woman's stuff lay strewn across the grass. There were a couple of oranges and a packet of *mealie* meal, some dresses and a few shirts. I went over to pick everything up. I held the clothes up to my face. They smelled strongly of Sunlight soap.

How often did this happen? Why hadn't I ever seen anything like it before? Probably because Mom had always driven me to school. She was so neurotic – even now, and I was fifteen for goodness sake – I'd only just managed to persuade her that no highwayman would swoop down and carry me off if I walked.

I checked my watch. Jeepers! It was late. Elise would be mad. We were supposed to meet at seven forty-five so we could walk to school together. I gathered the cloth and all the stuff into my arms, and hurried towards Elise's house.

I'd only joined the school four years before. That first break-time I'd stood against the wall, thin in my enormous uniform, plaits on either side of my face like bell pulls, my hands gripping the rough brickwork behind me. A pointy-chinned girl called Micheline, and her band of cronies, had hunted me down.

'You look about seven!' she'd sneered.

I didn't need to be reminded. Not only was I small for my age, but I'd also skipped a year in my previous school. 'I'm eleven,' I'd said. My voice came out like a bleat.

'She's not even twelve yet!' Micheline had jerked her head, and she and her gang had moved off. 'Baby!' she'd called out. 'Don't do anything in your *broekies*!'

'Take no notice,' someone said.

I'd thought I was alone. I wiped my snot on my blazer sleeve. A smallish round girl stood in front of me. Sunlight winked off her glasses.

'I'm Elise. *They* call me Two Ton – you know, like Two-Ton Tessie – or sometimes just *Vetsak*.' She took my arm. 'Come with me. I'll show you around.'

She'd seemed just like me – we'd both loved Jane Austen, we'd played never-ending games of tennis on her court and we'd boiled gallons of fudge together. But in the last year, ever since she'd got rid of her glasses and lost masses of weight, she'd begun to change. She wanted to be just like Micheline and most of the other girls in the class, and she was getting there – fast. Now I never knew what kind of mood she'd be in, and all we seemed to have in common was the road we both lived on. But she was the closest thing I had to a friend, and I kept hoping she would change back.

She was waiting for me outside her front gate.

'You're late, Victoria!' she said, tapping her watch. 'I thought you wanted to get to school early today!'

'I know,' I said. 'I do.' I was still feeling shaky.

'And what are you doing with all that rubbish?'

The black woman's belongings were spilling out of my arms. I knelt on the ground, trying to pack everything back into the cloth.

'I've just seen something really terrible, Elise. I saw

an old black lady being beaten and picked up by the police. She dropped her bundle. These are her things.'

'Well, she probably stole them anyway. Serves her right.'

'That's a horrible thing to say!'

Elise shrugged. She pulled her socks up to her knees, then rolled them down below her ankles.

'Chuck that junk away, and let's go,' she said.

I looked at the bundle. 'It's not junk, Elise! It's her stuff. She might come back for it.' I tightened the knots I'd made in the cloth. 'I think I'll just go back and put it under the hedge in case she does.'

'Oh, shut up about that woman. Look – you haven't seen me all holiday – what's different?' Elise asked. She put her hands on her hips and flung her hair about. It flew away from her head in a glossy arc, then landed neatly in a tucked-under roll around her face.

'Could it be your hair, by any chance?'

'It's called a pageboy. I had it done in London. Everyone's got their hair like this over there.' She grabbed my plait. 'I'm sure it'll come to South Africa soon. Then you can have yours done too.' She cocked her head, and nodded. 'You're always so old-fashioned, Victoria! We definitely need to do something about your look. And your long hair makes you look even more babyish.'

Typical Elise – making me feel like some kind of

freak. Well, whatever she said, there was no way I was going near a hairdresser. I jerked away from her.

'Do you think she's gone to jail?' I asked. I couldn't get the black woman out of my mind.

'Who? Oh – you're not still droning on about that black!' Elise put both her hands on the back of my satchel. 'Hurry up, Victoria! Let's sit at the back this term. Then I can spy on Craig.' She gave me a shove.

Of course, with my bag so stuffed I lost my balance, and I ended up on my knees.

'Elise! What d'you do that for?'

She didn't answer. She'd pushed her tongue into her cheek and, in a little mirror, was examining a green-headed pimple that shone out of her face. As I got to my feet she clicked the mirror shut, pushed it into her blazer pocket and marched off.

'Hurry!' she said over her shoulder.

I let her go ahead. I suddenly didn't care which desk I ended up with.

Chapter Two

A few days later I was sitting on the steps that fanned out from our front door down to the gravel drive. The sky was a wide-open blue. Another hot Sunday. Somewhere a dog was barking half-heartedly, and there were locusts bouncing in the grass. I scooped up another handful of pine needles and bent one into a loop. I'd never yet managed a chain of more than twenty.

The gravel crackled. Who was arriving this early?

Every Sunday we had 'open house'. People began to arrive at about eight o'clock in the morning, and came and went in relays throughout the day – though usually only when it was hot and sunny.

A car approached. It glittered in the early-morning sunshine.

'Do you like our new Jag?' a shrill voice called from the open window.

Oh no – not the Conways – too late to warn Mom.

Mrs Conway swung her legs out of the car. What

was she wearing? A yellow catsuit clung all the way to her knees and then exploded into yellow, black and white striped flares. They swished as she rocked across the soft grass in her six-inch heels. She'd unzipped the cat suit to her bosom and the huge circular zip pull tinkled like a cowbell. It grew fainter as she turned the corner of the house and made her way to the back garden. Talk about mutton dressed as lamb. Though Dad always said I shouldn't mock – especially not the Conways. Dr Conway sent him loads of patients.

I felt a puff of hot air on my neck. Dr Conway was leaning over me. I'd been so busy looking at his wife that I hadn't noticed him getting out of the car. He was so close I could count the bristles on the end of his strawberry nose.

'Tell your girl there's a bit of meat on the back seat,' he said. He smacked his red lips together. 'Lovely.'

. Backing away, I dropped the pine needles and leaped up the steps.

'Dad's by the pool,' I called over my shoulder. I heard again the black woman's hymn, the roar of the jeep, her cry, the slap, and the slam of the doors. 'Show some respect,' I muttered, half hoping he could hear me. 'Seraphina's not a "girl".' Why didn't I have the guts to say it out loud?

I waited inside until I was sure Dr Conway had moved off. The stones jabbed my bare feet as I made my way back over the gravel to his car. I opened the door. Bit of meat? More like half a cow. A huge package slumped in a heap. Blood was seeping through the brown-paper wrapping and pooling on the plastic tray beneath it. Flies snarled above it. I carried the tray to the patio at the back of the house, holding it as far away from me as possible and gulping air through my mouth. Dr Conway was hovering near Dad, who was lighting the barbecue.

'Dad!' I called.

He saw me struggling with the tray.

'Thanks, Victoria,' he said. He strode over and carried the meat to a table nearby. He knew how I felt about blood and meat.

'*Braaivleis*, rugby, sunny skies and Chevrolet – that advert certainly got it right,' Dr Conway said. He was rummaging in the front pockets of his towelling shirt.

Dad put his arm around me, and looked around. 'This is God's country,' he said.

'That's what I like to hear!' Dr Conway bent over the barbecue to light the cigar he'd been looking for, and found, in his pocket. 'Michael – you and I need to have a chat. I have a proposition for you.'

He slapped Dad on the back and pottered off to the poolside. Dr Conway gave me the creeps. Ever since he'd brushed his belly against me in the pool a month or two before – four times, so I knew it wasn't an accident – I'd tried to avoid him. And I'd felt his beady eyes watching me when I'd climbed out. Now he flickered his fingers at me in a little wave before pulling off his shorts. He pinged the waist of the tiny orange Speedo swimming costume he was wearing underneath.

'Come and join me, Victoria!'

A fat varicose vein snaked across his shin. Jeepers! I felt like vomiting. I felt more comfortable standing next to the slab of dead cow than I would venturing anywhere near him. He plopped into the water and swam a couple of lengths.

A wail coming from the house grew louder and louder. Charlie, my baby brother, had woken up. Soon Mom was making her way across the grass, with him clinging round her neck. Her long hair had slipped out of her hair slide. Her face was flushed and her left cheek was creased in a scalloped pattern.

'I could have slept forever,' she said. 'Hello, Cyril . . . Marguerite.'

Mrs Conway peered at Mom over her sunglasses. I knew she was taking in Mom's calloused bare feet and her crumpled, home-made skirt held together at the waist by a nappy pin. Sometimes she embarrassed me. Some of the girls in my class called her a hippy. But as Mrs Conway took a tissue out of her bag and patted her stippled armpits, I felt proud of Mom. I looked again at the diamonds that sparkled at Mrs Conway's ears, neck and fingers. She looked like a constellation. Spoilt old bag.

13

My brother was still crying. 'Michael!' Mom called. 'Could you just hold Charlie a minute while I make up a bottle?' But Dad had gone to greet some other guests.

Dr Conway meanwhile had pulled himself out of the water and plonked his walnut-tanned, barrel-chested mass into a deckchair. He put his hands to his ears. 'Can't you get the girl to take him?' he asked. He leered at Mom. 'Then you can come and sit next to me, Joanna, and we can have a nice quiet chat.'

'*I'm* the girl!' I muttered, but not loudly enough for him to hear. I put my arms out for my brother. 'Come, Charlie. Come with me. I'll get his bottle, Mom.'

'I can't believe how grown up she is now!' I heard Dr Conway say as I headed off.

The back of the house was dark and cool. An old tree held its limbs over the backyard. Its shade was a haven. Charlie stopped crying and wound his hands through my hair.

'Let's go inside and get your drink,' I murmured. I stopped to wipe the dusty soles of my feet on the sides of my legs. There was a movement from the tree over-head. I jerked. There was a dark shape crouching on one of the branches.

'Maswe! What are you doing up there?'

The tree whined as Maswe sprang. He landed silently on all fours. He arched his back and straight-ened up. I hadn't seen him for two years. He'd been only a bit taller than me then. Now I had to shade my eyes as I looked up at him. He took a bit of wood he'd been chewing out from between his teeth.

'Come,' he said, and pulled me by my sleeve through the backyard and out to the path at the side of the house. It was even cooler there. The sun never really managed to poke its way through to that part of the garden. I shivered a little and pulled Charlie closer to me.

'Maswe – what a surprise! How's college? I know it's far away, but why haven't you come to see us before?' I asked. 'Hasn't your term begun yet? How long will you be staying?'

He waved his hand, swatting away my questions. He gave off a spicy smell of cumin-scented fresh sweat and eucalyptus. I'd seen the photo of his father on Seraphina's bookshelf; Maswe had begun to look just like him. His cheeks were scooped out, and now there were straight angles where there used to be boyish roundness. That, and the beard of closely set burrs around the point of his chin, made him look much older than nineteen. His eyes darted about, never resting. He seemed barely aware of me and Charlie.

'Where is my mother?' he asked.

'She's at church. She'll be back in a few hours.' Suddenly I didn't know how to talk to him. I felt shy. 'Shall I tell my parents you're here?' Jeepers – why did I sound so formal?

For the first time Maswe focused his gaze on me. He put his arm out as if to block me. 'No,' he said. He frowned.

I shifted Charlie on to my hip. Maswe and I had played together when we were little. When I'd been only a bit older than Charlie, Maswe had carried me on his back at top speed round the garden of the house we used to live in. There were probably still traces of the sunflowers we'd painted on the door to Seraphina's old room. I wasn't frightened, but I was surprised by his tone.

'Maswe—'

'Sorry, Tori,' he said, and his face split into his old Chiclet-toothed smile. 'Tori' was his nickname for me. 'I need some money,' he said, slinging a stained canvas bag across his back. He knelt to tie his shoelaces. He was not wearing socks. The tendons at his heels were tight and sharp, the skin burnished smooth.

'I've got quite a bit. Maybe ten rand. Are you going back to college now?'

Maswe shook his head and stood up. 'The money, Tori. Quick!' he said.

With Charlie bouncing against me, I scrambled up the back stairs and into the house. I tipped Charlie into his cot and raced to my bedroom. Emptying my money box, I tore back through the house and outside again.

'Maswe?'

His lean silhouette flitted in and out of the dappled shade.

'I've got twelve rand!' I said, running up behind him, spilling a few coins in the sand. I bent to pick them up.

Maswe stopped. 'Thanks, Tori.' He smiled again. He hadn't lost the deep dimple in his right cheek. He placed a hand on my shoulder and then carried on down the path.

'Go carefully, Maswe,' I said. He waved without turning round. I inhaled sharply. I could still feel the heat from his hand on my shoulder. After a few seconds I ran to the end of the path and looked up and down the road. He'd disappeared. I stood for a moment. A car drove past, leaving a jangle of pop music hanging in the air.

I felt a strange tang of sadness and elation. Making my way back to the house, I pressed my bare feet into the whirled shoe prints left behind by Maswe.

Chapter Three

'Victoria, what's got into you?' Elise whined.

It was the next day. We were walking home after school. Elise trailed behind me, and when I looked back I could see her stopping to hitch up the waistband of her skirt.

'You've been weird all day.'

I speeded up. 'Get a move on, Elise! And stop lifting up your uniform. I've seen enough of your *broekies* for one day.'

'Whoo – someone got out of bed the wrong side. First, you stared out of the window for the whole of English.' She counted the incidents off on her fingers. 'Then, you ignored dear, sweet little Miss Obers. Then you completely disappeared at break-time—'

'You knew I had to help in the library.' I spun round and began to walk backwards. 'And talking about weird behaviour – what were you doing with Micheline and all her gang, sitting against the wall with your socks rolled down and your skirt rolled up? Not so long ago you said you wouldn't be seen dead with that lot.'

Elise shrugged. She gave a half-smile, slow and subtle as a lizard's.

'Maybe they aren't as bad as we thought.'

'I never thought I'd hear you say that.' I turned again and stomped ahead. I reached Elise's house. For a moment I hesitated. Usually we carried on talking at the gate, or I'd go in for a cold drink. Well, for once I wasn't going to do that.

'You're just jealous, Victoria!' Elise called out. 'Because Miche likes me.'

As soon as I heard Elise's gate clack shut behind me, I slowed down.

'I'm not jealous!' I yelled.

Micheline and her cronies were sly and shallow. Why would I want to be one of them? Discovering my best friend among them still stung. And even worse – she'd blended in with them perfectly.

As I opened our side gate I noticed that nothing remained of Maswe's footprints. I trudged down the path and into the backyard. Seraphina's door was closed. Charlie's nappies drooped from the washing line. There was no sign of Hattie, the dog. I hadn't seen her since the day before. In the kitchen, a bowl of cake batter had been abandoned. A breeze rustled the open pages of a recipe book.

'Mom!'

'Is that you, darling?' Mom padded into the kitchen just as I plunged a finger into the cake mix and licked it. 'You'll get worms!' she laughed.

'I'm not four, Mom. I don't believe those stories any more.' I shrugged off my satchel and flung it down.

'Shall I put this in your room?' Mom asked, stooping to pick up my satchel.

'No, just leave it!' I snapped. Mom's face slackened with hurt. 'Sorry – I-I'll take it myself.'

'Darling,' Mom said, stirring the mixture, 'Dad's got late surgery this evening. He won't be here for dinner. So – more chocolate cake for us.' She leaned towards me and nuzzled my hair. 'Why don't you have a rest before you do your homework? You seem a bit tired.' She poured the batter into a tin and put it into the oven. 'That's Charlie crying. Perfect timing.' She left me slouched against the kitchen counter.

'Why does she always have to be so understanding?' I muttered. Immediately I felt another rush of guilt. After all, she could have been really vile, like Elise's mother.

Wandering out to the back door, I felt again the shadow of the tree that overhung the backyard. I thought I would tell Seraphina that Maswe had been round.

I had to knock three times before Seraphina opened her door. Her headscarf was pushed far back off her forehead; puffs of greying hair sprang around her face.

'I'm sorry, Seraphina. Were you asleep?'

'Come in, my child. I was not sleeping.' She rubbed her eyes with the heels of her hands, then plucked at the headscarf, trying to draw it back into place.

I'd always loved visiting Seraphina in her room. I loved the nostril-searing smell of camphor cream and the warm fragrance of ironed, starched clothes. Seraphina's bed was raised on bricks to ward off the tokoloshe – an evil, shadowy spirit who preyed on women. I climbed on to the bed and leaned against the wall.

'*Hau!*' Seraphina sighed as she folded her tall frame into the armchair. She was holding a piece of paper.

'Is that a letter from your sister?'

Letters from Esther always made Seraphina feel tired, and I could see fatigue in the slope of her shoulders and the angle of her neck.

Seraphina wiped her face upward, her long fingers coming to rest across her forehead.

'No,' she replied, 'it is not.'

She folded the letter quickly, but not before I'd managed to read the letterhead: 'The Betsy Longacre Foundation'. It was from Maswe's college. I had also caught the scraps of a sentence: 'non-attendance . . . distracted behaviour . . . regret to inform . . .'

'Is it about Maswe?' I asked, although I knew the answer.

Seraphina did not reply. She tucked the letter down

21

the front of her uniform and sighed again. It was a ragged sound. I sensed that she was close to tears.

I'd never known Seraphina to cry. She'd always had a way of lifting her chin and kind of soaking up her sorrows. Especially after all the business with Maswe's father. I'd heard Mom call him a freewheeling, hard-drinking, good-for-nothing. No one had told me exactly how he'd died, but I'd pieced together a story about a knifing behind Boetie's Bottle Store. Maswe was Seraphina's only child. Mom always said Seraphina had poured all her hope into him. She was terrified that Maswe might turn into his father. Seraphina would be so upset if she knew just how far from college Maswe really was. How could I tell her that he'd been round the afternoon before?

Seraphina shook her head. She then glanced at the upside-down nurse's watch pinned to her uniform.

'Time to make supper.'

She pushed on the arms of the chair to raise herself and took an apron from a stack on her dressing table. It crackled as she ducked her head into it and tied it at her back.

'And time for your homework, my child.'

Her footsteps were slow as she scuff-scuffed up the steps and through the back door into the house.

I sat for a few minutes longer on Seraphina's bed. I could trace my life in the things she'd arranged around the room. A doll I'd loved until it became bald had been saved from the bin by Seraphina. It now sat on a shelf next to my first pair of shoes. On the wall, Seraphina had sticky-taped Maswe's and my handprints and sloppy paintings. There was a small wooden bookcase next to her bed. Her Bible was on the top shelf, balancing on her hymn book. She'd marked the place in each with a flattened Lux soap wrapper. On the lower shelves she'd arranged twenty or thirty photographs. Some of these were yellowing sepia portraits of stiff-backed relatives – like the one of Maswe's father – but mostly they were bright pictures of me and my parents, my granny, Maswe and, more recently, of Charlie.

'Better go,' I muttered to myself.

As I jumped off the bed an unframed photograph fluttered to the floor. I picked it up. It was a slightly blurred picture of Maswe. I'd taken it on the day he'd left for college. We'd both been laughing at the suitcase full of cakes and biscuits Granny had baked for him. I brought the photo closer to my face, trying to trace the Maswe I'd seen the day before in the uncomplicated smile caught by the camera. I put it back on the shelf and left Seraphina's room. I was about to shut the door behind me when I stopped. I went back into the room, grabbed the photograph and slid it into my pocket.

Chapter Four

'Come on, lovey. Get in. I was just passing the school, and I thought, as it's Friday, I'd give you girls a lift home.'

I'd spotted Elise's mother's car from the classroom. It wasn't easy to miss. It was probably the only shocking-pink Mercedes in South Africa.

'I know you two have had some sort of tiff.' Elise's mother poked her head out of the car window. She spoke in a wheedling tone. 'Hop in, have a cold drink by us and you can sort it out, hey?'

I'd managed to avoid having much to do with Elise all that week and the week before. I was tempted to ignore Elise's mother and stomp off to feast on my rage and upset a bit longer. But, on the other hand, it was becoming boring secreting myself in the library every lunch break. And I missed Elise. She was already sitting in the back of the car. She caught my eye and gave a conspiratorial grimace.

'Oh, thank you, Mrs Westcott.'

'No – not in the front, lovey!' Elise's mother shrieked as I opened the front passenger door. 'My party wig's just been to the hairdresser. You'll mess it up! And how many times have I asked you to call me Auntie Beulah, hey?'

She looked like a doll – some spoilt child's favourite, fat doll. She wore bow-embellished tent dresses all day and, according to Elise, all night.

Elise's mother leaned across the back of the seat to lock the door, her loose bosom rolling about under the chiffon. Then with three jerks she reversed and sped over the bumpy track and out through the school gates. The party wig on its polystyrene head and long neck teetered about on the passenger seat.

Go on, drop! I willed silently. Fall over!

Out of the corner of my eye I could see Elise doing the same. We were both snorting with laughter when we got out of the car.

'Friends again – that's better, hey?' Elise's mother said as she opened the front door. 'Agnes – I'm back!'

The maid was hovering in the hallway, wiping her hands on her apron.

'Agnes, the shopping's in the boot!' she called out. 'And be careful with my wig.'

Elise dragged me into her bedroom. We fell against each other in hysterics.

'I just knew what you were thinking,' Elise said.

'Imagine what it looked like through the window!' A huge snort rose to the surface again.

'Don't . . .' Elise laughed. 'You're the only person who can make me laugh like this.'

I knew that that was the closest Elise would get to apologizing. 'Hey, Victoria, look at this. I got it in London.' She leaped to her wardrobe and pulled out a fringed suede skirt and waistcoat. 'And this.' She flung a floaty garment across the bed.

'Where did you get *that*?' I asked. I pointed at a gold heart pendant, ringed with rubies, which had flipped out of the neck of Elise's school shirt.

'Shh. It's my mom's. She'd have a fit if she knew I'd borrowed it.' She held it to the window so that the sun flashed red geometry across the walls. 'Daddy bought it for their anniversary.'

Mom wouldn't have known what to do with something like that pendant. Dad had bought her some old maps of South Africa for *their* anniversary.

'Victoria – wake up! I said try these on!' Elise was flapping some clothes at me.

'No – they won't suit me.'

'Get on with it. I told you I was going to do something about your look.'

Struggling to pull my school shirt over my head I heard a rasp as something fluttered out of the pocket. It was the photo of Maswe.

'What's this, Victoria?' Elise had picked it up.

26

'Could this be a picture of your secret boyfriend?' She held it high up above her head, dancing away from my grabbing hands.

'Elise – give it back!'

Elise leaped on to her bed. 'Let's see if it's someone I know.'

'Elise – I said give it back!' I scrambled on to the bed and reached out again. Gripping the photo, Elise turned it over.

'Oh – it's only some black,' she said, and flicked the photograph on to the floor. 'Hey, wait a minute . . . why are you carrying a photo of a black boy?'

'It's Seraphina's son. I took the photo for her when he left for college.' I felt the hot stain of a blush creep up my neck. 'I've only just had the film developed.' The lie coiled from my mouth like a snake unwinding. 'I wanted to surprise her with it when she washed my shirt.' I picked up the picture and put it back in my pocket.

Elise seemed to have lost interest in the photo. 'I'm glad he's gone.' She wrinkled her nose. 'You spent so much time with that native boy you began to stink like a black. Anyway, I can't wait to see what you look like in this.'

I knew I would have to allow Elise to dress me up and rearrange my hair. She was singing a pop song as she rummaged in a drawer for hairslides. I sat in front of her dressing table, trying to avoid my reflection. I was ashamed at having lied. I had betrayed Maswe.

Elise began to fiddle with my hair, draping it one way, then another. The hairpins she was trying to thread into it speared my scalp. I let Elise finish her remodelling. But before I was allowed back into my school uniform, Elise made me go into her mother's room so that she could admire her handiwork.

'Come, let Auntie Beulah see.' She was lying in the middle of her bed, camouflaged among the pink flounces. She rolled herself upright. 'Ach, shame, man! You look so cute!' she said, and pressed her rosebud lips to my forehead.

It was dusk by the time I left Elise's house. I felt tired and somehow wrong-footed. I thought again of Maswe's panther-like drop from the tree and checked my pocket to make sure the photo was safe. A chill breeze slunk through the roadside hedges and rattled the leaves. Overhead, a seagull let out a pleading mew. Tears pricked my eyes.

Chapter Five

I dragged the sleeve of my blazer across my eyes before going into the house. Seraphina was feeding Charlie in the kitchen.

'You are late. I was beginning to worry,' Seraphina said, mirroring Charlie's open mouth. 'You promised Miss Joanna you'd be back by six o'clock.'

'Sorry, Seraphina. I should have phoned. I was at Elise's house.'

'What have you done to your hair, my child?'

'Elise did it.' I began to rake through my hair, tearing the clips and pins out. 'Are Mom and Dad here?'

'Miss Joanna and the Doctor have gone out for dinner. With Dr Conway and his wife.'

I kissed Charlie and rubbed my nose in his hair.

'Poor Mom and Dad! Dr Conway gives me the creeps, and his wife's—'

'No more of that, Victoria.' Seraphina frowned. She did not like disrespectful behaviour. 'Your food is nearly ready!' she called after me as I left the kitchen.

My bedroom had once been Dad's study. The wrapping-paper-brown hessian curtains he'd chosen made the room masculine and sober. I'd always liked that. Especially after an afternoon in Elise's frilly, floral boudoir. I threw myself backwards on to my bed and watched the light dimming in each window grid.

The splash of gravel and a yellow headlight beam startled me.

Mom and Dad back early? I thought I'd heard their usual homecoming sounds, so I was surprised to hear the drone of the front door bell. 'Must have left their keys behind.'

I ran to open the front door. A policeman was standing there.

'Sergeant Kloete.' His voice was coarse, thickened by phlegm. He stepped into the hall. His boots rang on the tiled floor. 'I found this there over by the Location,' he said, lifting his arm.

It was only then that I noticed Hattie, held by the scruff in his hand like a bag of shopping. The dog scrabbled and paddled her legs. She could hardly even whimper – there was no slack left in her neck.

'Hattie!' I lunged towards her, but the policeman swung Hattie out of my reach. His knuckles were bruised. A huge cross was tattooed on the back of his hand. I drew back.

'You want to look after your property, *meisie*,' he said. 'Kaffirs eat dogs, you know.' He cleared his throat. 'Specially the blacks there by the Location.' He smiled. His front teeth were smaller than his canines. He opened his hand. Hattie landed in a heap. She whined softly, and half slid, half scuttled out of the entrance hall.

The policeman took off his hat. He twisted his bull neck to look at the paintings and furniture. '*Ja*,' he said, and nodded, giving Dad's collection of South African art his approval. He strode over to one of the maps Dad had given Mom for their anniversary. Flexing his hand for a moment, he tapped the glass with his thumb. I had never seen such a long nail on a man. '*My land*. My country,' he said. Pride made his voice gruff.

I could hear Seraphina coming down the passage. I knew how suspicious and frightened of the police she was: she'd had enough to do with them when her husband was alive.

'Who's there, Victoria?' she called.

Why wouldn't he leave? I willed him to go before Seraphina got there, but he remained planted in front of the map.

Sergeant Kloete cleared another fruity clot from the back of his throat. 'Good evening, Mrs Salwise,' he said, without turning, as Seraphina appeared. 'And how is your son – Maswe?'

'*Hau!*' Seraphina gasped.

I was as surprised as Seraphina that the policeman

knew who she was, and just as shocked by his mentioning Maswe by name. I shivered.

'Is there anything else?' I asked. I tried to be as polite as possible.

'*Ja.*' He swung round and settled his hat between his jutting ears. 'Tell Dr Miller it was Sergeant Kloete who saved his Hettie's life.' The belt around his middle was tight, the gleam of its buckle danced light around the walls. At his hip was a big black gun. Tapping it with the long thumbnail, he added, 'And tell the Doctor congratulations on his new post. We is very pleased to have him on board.'

He strode over to the front door and pulled it shut behind him. I listened to the staccato ring of his boots as he trotted down the front steps. What did he mean by Dad's 'new post'? And how did he know Seraphina and, even more worrying, Maswe? I remembered the letter from Maswe's college. I hoped he wasn't in some sort of trouble.

Chapter Six

The next morning, Saturday, Charlie woke me up. Mom was holding him over me as he patted me and dripped drool on to my face.

'Charlie!' I moaned, burrowing into my pillow.

'Morning, sweetie,' Mom said. 'I haven't seen you since yesterday morning.' She gathered up a few strands of my hair and tucked them behind my ear. 'Seraphina's made crumpets. Come and get some while they're still hot.'

Mom and Dad and Charlie were already outside on the patio, having breakfast, when I appeared. It was a golden morning.

'Good morning, sleepyhead,' Dad said, reaching out and hugging me as I passed. He smelled of toothpaste and coffee. His thick hair hadn't yet been flattened by the Brylcreem he combed into it every day; it stood on end. Usually this made me smile, but I'd slept so badly I just felt irritable. I was still bothered by

Kloete's visit the evening before. I huddled into my dressing gown.

Dad rocked back in his chair, stretched out his arms and tilted his face to the sun. 'At long last, a whole Saturday off—'

'Dad,' I interrupted him, 'do the police know everything about us?'

'Oh, Victoria – of course not!' As he hadn't shaved, there was a blue Fred Flintstone shadow round his mouth and chin. He scratched at his face lazily, then poured syrup over his plate of crumpets. He obviously wasn't paying attention to what I was saying.

'Well, Sergeant Kloete seemed to. He knew Seraphina's name. And he knew ours.' I screwed up my eyes against the light bouncing off the coffee pot on the table.

'Who is Sergeant Kloete, darling?' Mom asked.

At least *someone* was listening. I described the policeman's visit.

'Oh, he's probably an ambitious young policeman, keen to impress,' Dad said.

'And he said something about "having you on board" and a new job.' I swatted a wasp away from my breakfast. 'You haven't got a new job, have you, Dad?'

'Doesn't news travel fast in a small town! Cyril Conway asked me last night whether I wanted to be his Assistant District Surgeon. I haven't actually agreed to do it yet. But –' he smiled – 'I probably will.'

'District Surgeon . . . ?' I was puzzled. 'But how did that policeman know about that, and what's it got to do with the police anyway? You won't be working for the police, will you?'

Seraphina had come out of the house with Charlie's cereal. She stopped dead when she heard what I'd just said, and clapped her hand to her mouth.

'No, darling. Daddy would be working for the Government,' Mom explained. 'Looking after prisoners would be only one of his duties.'

Dad smiled again. 'I feel . . .' He searched for the right words. 'I would feel proud to be doing something for my country,' he said. He stretched, then rolled his napkin into its ring. 'Thank you for breakfast, Seraphina.'

I couldn't believe how casual my parents were about Sergeant Kloete's visit. I was desperate to get their attention. 'And he had the most hideous long talon of a thumbnail,' I continued. 'Didn't he, Seraphina?'

'I expect he plays the guitar, darling,' Mom said. 'Now, as soon as Seraphina's ready, we're off to the Location. Sarie Potgieter's away this week, so I'm on duty at the soup kitchen. We'll only be gone a few hours.' She passed Charlie over to Dad. 'What are you up to, Victoria?'

'I'm coming with you.' I leaped up. 'Wait for me to get dressed.'

*

35

'Please, Miss Joanna – I'm not happy in the front,' Seraphina said as she tried to edge past Mom to get into the back of the car. 'I am afraid of trouble.'

I knew she meant trouble with the police.

'Nonsense, Seraphina. There won't be any trouble.' Mom held the front passenger door open for her. She waited until Seraphina was installed, then she and I wedged the pot of soup between the rear and the front seats. 'Victoria, I won't drive fast, but keep your hands on the lid anyway. I don't want it to splosh out.'

The conversation at breakfast was still bothering me. The visit to the soup kitchen would take my mind off it. I was also curious: I'd never been to either the Location or the soup kitchen before.

We drove slowly, past white shadow-dappled houses with emerald lawns, the morning hush interrupted now and then by the spurt of sprinklers. After a while the houses seemed to fall away and we entered an industrial area with deserted warehouses and abandoned garages. There were hardly any trees, but the few that there were looked dusty and derelict.

The car shuddered as the tarred road crumbled into loose sand and chunks of stone. We passed through some high rusty gates and bumped on to a dirt track.

'Are we in the Location now?' I asked.

'Yes, darling. The soup kitchen isn't very far from here.'

Black people were coming and going, most of them

36

women, with cloth bundles on their heads. They stopped to let the car past, staring through the windows at us.

'What they must think of me, sitting here like the Queen of Sheba,' Seraphina mumbled, trying to shrink lower into her seat.

Mom patted Seraphina's arm. 'We're almost there. Hang on to that lid, Victoria!'

She steered the car down the deeply rutted stony track. On either side there stretched a never-ending expanse of tumbledown shacks. Most were small, misshapen heaps of metal and cardboard – patchworked stop signs, old advertising stuff, fruit boxes and other discarded bits and pieces. It would only take a sneeze to flatten them. Children ran in and out of these ramshackle huts. Most of them were barefoot and half naked. There were flies everywhere – clotted like jam under the children's noses and in dark clouds above their heads. A few stringy chickens pottered about, scratching in the orange-coloured dirt. We were only about twenty minutes' drive from home, but it felt like a million miles away.

'I didn't realize the Location would be like this,' I said. If Maswe weren't back at college, maybe I'd see him here, and a bubble of hope fizzed inside me. I looked closely at the people as they passed. There were very few young men around. 'Everyone's either a child or old,' I said out loud. 'Where are all the young people?'

'The young people are working,' Seraphina said. 'Those who cannot sleep at their place of work come back here at night.'

'Where's your house, Seraphina?'

'It is ten minutes from the bus station. I am lucky. I do not live in a tin hut.' She looked at Mom. 'Every time I step into my brick house, I say thank you to the Lord and Miss Joanna and the Doctor.'

'Does Maswe ever stay there?' I asked. I'd been rolling Maswe's name around in my mouth, desperate to say it out loud. But it had come out too loud and too stark. I glanced at Mom and Seraphina. Neither seemed to have noticed.

'Sometimes Maswe comes,' Seraphina said, her head bowed. I knew she was thinking about the letter from Maswe's college, and I was sorry that I'd reminded her of his truancy.

The car juddered to a halt outside a corrugated-iron shed painted bright blue. A gaggle of children gathered round the car. 'Miss Joanna! Miss Joanna!' they shouted, pushing to be the first to greet her. They were all carrying containers – some were plastic cups or bowls, some were old tin cans with jagged edges.

'We're later than usual,' Mom said, looking at her watch. 'They're hungry. Come, Victoria – let's get the soup out.'

I climbed out of the car. There was a sudden hush.

'This is Victoria. Don't be frightened. She's my daughter.'

Seraphina then said something in her own language, and the children began their clamour again. A few little girls moved over to stand beside me. One of them reached out to touch my shorts; another skimmed her hand over the surface of my hair.

Mom unlocked the door to the shed.

'This doubles up as the school during the week,' she explained. There was an old easel blackboard leaning against one of the walls and a few battered books stacked in the corner. I recognized some of them. They had once been mine.

'Victoria, give Seraphina a hand with the trestle table. It needs to be dragged outside.'

Mom got on with lighting the Primus stove. She set the soup on it to heat. More children came running from all directions, clutching their vessels. Soon they'd made a line that began at the table and wiggled down the main dirt track almost further than I could see.

'Wow! There are so many children,' I said to Seraphina. 'Will there be enough soup for them all?'

Chapter Seven

I held the ladle up, ready to pour. Instead of a container being held out, there was a pair of cupped hands. A boy of about seven stood in front of me. He had a baby clamped around his body.

'Where is your bowl?' I asked.

The boy shook his head. Some flies flew out.

'Seraphina, is there a bowl for this little boy?'

'There are no more spare bowls,' Seraphina replied. She said something to the boy. He ambled off, the baby still clinging to him.

'There must be something we can use,' I said. 'Wait a minute – there's Charlie's drinking cup in the car!'

I found it on the back ledge and raced down the track. The boy had disappeared.

I wished I'd asked his name. Then I would have been able to call him. Half walking, half trotting, I made my way down the alleys that criss-crossed the Location, peering into the dwellings.

Heat flashed off the tin shacks. Without any trees,

40

there was no shade. Sound was amplified in the flat, sun-beaten landscape: there was the clatter of corrugated iron as elderly women struggled to put up more structures, babies were crying, children yelling. On one corner a woman was standing in her underwear, screaming at someone I couldn't see. From time to time the mangy dog at her feet joined in with a manic bark. Further on, a couple of old men sprawled in the sun, hats over their faces, lager cans in their hands, the radio they'd parked between them roaring out pop music. The smells of cooking and sewage fought with each other, and the sewage was winning.

As I passed, people stared. I could feel eyes gazing out at me from behind every patchwork hut. It was useless. I realized that I'd never find him. Lowering my head, I decided to go back to Mom and Seraphina.

As I turned to retrace my steps, I caught sight of someone lean and tall flitting between two huts about fifty metres away.

'Maswe?'

Could it really be him? He'd shaken his head when I'd asked if he was going back to college. So it could be him. It had to be him. I'd have known his lanky silhouette and that loping, graceful movement anywhere. Maybe he was going to their house to surprise Seraphina. I began to run, deeper and deeper into the Location, dodging the children playing in the dirt and hopping over ditches.

41

'Maswe!' I tried to shout, but my throat was dry and I was panting too much. He had stopped to talk to someone. If only he'd wait just for a minute, just long enough for me to reach him.

'Maswe!' I yelled. He must have heard me. But he didn't even turn around.

A child laughed. I felt something sting my cheek.

'Ow!' I shouted. 'What was that?'

I stopped running and rubbed my face. There was another laugh. A boy of about five or six was standing on a pile of old tyres. His arm was raised, his fist clenched around a large stone.

'No!' I screamed. 'Stop throwing stones!'

I ducked as the boy hurled his next missile. With a clang, it hit a dustbin near to where I was standing. He bent down to scoop up a few more stones.

'Why are you throwing stones at me? I haven't done anything to you!'

The boy wasn't laughing now. His face was curled into a snarl. Shielding my head with my arm, I began to run again.

'Not so fast, missie.' Sergeant Kloete stood in front of me, his arms out, blocking my path. 'I saw what happened here.'

'No, no – it's fine. Nothing happened.' I tried to dodge past him. I needed to get away. I was losing Maswe.

42

Sergeant Kloete grabbed my shoulder. 'You were assaulted. I saw it with my own eyes.'

He strode over to the boy, who was cowering behind the dustbin.

'Come out of there, you little rat! You hit her with a stone, and now you must be punished.'

'No, no – I'm fine! He didn't do any harm!' I shouted.

Sergeant Kloete took no notice. He dragged the boy out from his hiding place by his shirt. He then swung his arm back and hit the child on the side of his head.

'No!' I yelled, just as the force of the policeman's blow flung the boy like a bundle of dirty washing against an upturned metal tub. After lying there stunned for a moment, he began to scream. I darted forward to help him, but I was pulled back by Sergeant Kloete.

'Leave him.' He wiped his hand on his trousers. 'That's the only language they understand. Lucky I was here.' He gave the boy a deft kick in the ribs. 'Shut up, or I will really give you something to cry about.'

I felt my skin prickle and then freeze. I began to shiver. My instinct was to start running again. As I turned away Sergeant Kloete grabbed my arm.

'*Wag 'n bietjie, meisie* – Wait a minute, miss. What's the rush?' His mouth was smiling, but his eyes were not. 'What are you doing here?'

'I thought I saw –' I blurted out. 'I mean – there was

43

a boy who came to the soup kitchen. But he didn't have a cup, so I ran after him to give him this one.' I waved Charlie's cup.

Sergeant Kloete didn't seem to be listening. 'You shouldn't be here. You are breaking the law.' He stepped closer to me. 'Don't you know how dangerous it is here, little white *meisie*? People get murdered, little white girl.' He said 'murdered' extra loudly. 'Soup kitchen, did you say? Let's get you back there. Make quick.' He gave me a shove. His long thumbnail stabbed my back. 'Bloody white liberals,' he muttered.

Mom was standing outside the soup kitchen. As soon as I saw her I felt a sob rise in my throat.

'Victoria, my darling! What's happened? Where've you been? Seraphina went to look for you.'

Sergeant Kloete took off his hat and reached out to shake Mom's hand. 'I am Sergeant Kloete, Mrs Miller. Pleased to make your acquaintance.' He coughed up a dry laugh. 'First I find the Miller dog in the Location, then I find the Miller daughter.'

Mom put her arm around me. 'Thank you on both counts, Sergeant Kloete,' she said.

'We're always glad to help.' Replacing his hat, he poked his head round the door of the soup kitchen. 'Smells good,' he said. Under his breath, I heard him add, 'Too good for piccanins.'

'Let's shout for Seraphina,' Mom said to me.

'Maybe she'll hear us. She needs to know that you're safe.'

'Here she is,' Sergeant Kloete said as Seraphina made her way towards us a few minutes later. She threw her arms open wide when she saw me.

'My child, you are safe.'

I hugged her. The back of her uniform was soggy with sweat.

'Sorry to break up the party,' Sergeant Kloete said. 'I should have given you this message for your son last night, Mrs Salwise.' He pronounced her name with a mocking exaggeration of a black person's accent. Leaning towards her, his nostrils flaring, he crushed one of his hands with the other so that the joints clicked. 'Tell Maswe, *pas op* – watch out.' He smiled. 'Good day.' He strode off back into the depths of the Location.

'Take no notice,' Mom said to Seraphina. 'He's just a bully.'

Seraphina remained silent. She climbed into the back of the car and sat there hunched over, her hands clasped to her chest. Nothing Mom or I could say would persuade her to sit in the front again. I knew that she was terrified of Sergeant Kloete. His parting warning had sent a chill down my spine too.

I'd been too shocked to tell Mom and Seraphina what Sergeant Kloete had done, and now I didn't want to make Seraphina even more distressed. Maswe was

45

obviously up to something, and the police were watching him. If it *had* been Maswe at least he'd got away.

I watched the dirty oranges and browns of the area around the Location melt into the jade greens and fresh whites of my own suburb.

When Hattie scuttled over the gravel to greet us, I buried my face in the soft folds around her neck and breathed in her warmed-mud smell.

Chapter Eight

'Darling, do you want to tell me what's wrong?' Mom sat next to me as I lay on my bed. She smoothed my hair away from my forehead.

'You've been miserable all week – ever since you came with me to the soup kitchen last Saturday. Perhaps you're coming down with something.' She pressed her cheek against my face. 'No temperature – but shall I ask Daddy to check you out?'

'No.' I pushed my mother away and buried my face in the crook of my arm. 'Just leave me alone. Please.'

Mom sighed. 'I don't like leaving you . . . You could bring a book, sit in the car if you want to.' She slipped her bag off her shoulder. 'Actually, I think we'll cancel our arrangement. I knew I should have asked Seraphina to stay. Michael—'

'No, Mom. Please go. I'll be fine. I just need some time to myself.' I sat up. I scraped my hair behind my ears and manufactured a bright smile. 'I've got loads of homework. It'll be good not to have any distractions.'

47

Undecided, Mom stood in the doorway for a moment. Then she slung her bag back over her shoulder. 'All right, darling. We'll go. Maybe even have a walk on the beach – if the weather holds. Charlie loves the sound of the sea. It'll help him to drop off. And then we'll be right back. All the doors are locked. Don't let anyone in. There's plenty of bread and salad in the fridge, and some cheesecake too.'

I listened to the grind of gravel as they drove off, then threw myself back on to my bed. It was true – ever since my visit to the Location the week before I'd been grumpy and horrible. Of course I was upset by the poverty I'd seen, and by Kloete's brutality. But I was really disappointed to have been so close to Maswe and then to have lost him. I felt a kind of curdled feeling in my chest that was a mixture of yearning and worry about Maswe's safety.

'Oh, stop being so pathetic, Victoria,' I muttered. I got off my bed and went over to the window. Hattie was in the garden. She was scampering about, now and then hurling herself upward in her heavy-boned way to snap at an insect.

'Oh, Hattie – you're bonkers!' I couldn't help smiling. I trotted through the house, unlocked the back door and ran into the garden.

'Hattie! Batty Hattie!' I called, and threw myself on to the grass, waiting to be attacked by paws and slobber.

But Hattie was now circling the overgrown tree stump which Maswe and I had called Big Bush. Maswe had discovered that we could bury ourselves inside its dense foliage and not be seen from the outside. We'd spent hours inside it once, watching Mom and Seraphina searching for us.

'Come on, Hattie!' I called again. Hattie had her nose to the ground and her backside in the air. She was yapping at Big Bush. 'What's your problem?' I got up and wandered over to her.

I heard a groan, and the leaves of the bush began to churn. There was a cracking of branches as someone crashed through the bush's mesh and on to the ground. Hattie growled and I screamed.

'Victoria –'

'Maswe?' I drew closer. 'Maswe! You keep dropping out of trees!'

I laughed with relief and happiness and tugged at his arm to pull him out of the tangle of twigs. When he drew breath sharply and moaned I let go of him.

'Maswe – you're hurt! What's happened? Have you been in a fight?'

Shaking his head, he turned away from me, withdrawing into the hood of his jacket. His breathing was shallow and laboured. He put his hand to his ribcage.

'Let's get you into the house.' I reached out,

brushing his shoulder with my fingertips. 'Don't worry – Dad will be home soon. He'll sort you out.'

'No! Must hide. Tell nobody I am here.' He anticipated my next question. 'Not even my mother. Dangerous for her.'

He tried to disentangle his legs from the bush. I dug my hands into the foliage and wrenched an opening in it.

'Hide me. Quick,' he said.

I looked around. Where could I hide him? A cold wind had sprung up, the sky had bruised over and it was beginning to rain. I had to get him under shelter quickly.

'I know – old maid's room. Let's go.'

I tried to help him to his knees. He couldn't stand. His ankles were swollen; they couldn't support his weight. I crawled along beside him. When he sank to the ground, I waited until he'd gathered enough strength to continue. Hattie was dancing about, licking Maswe and barking. I swiped at her to stop, but it only made her more excited. The rain was now heavy and Mom and Dad were likely to return at any minute. I began to panic.

The old servant's room had been built in the 1920s, quite far from the main house, in a part of the garden that had not yet been tamed. Because the plumbing in the old quarters had been primitive and the room poky,

50

Dad had had a new room and bathroom built for Seraphina across the backyard.

'We're almost there,' I murmured. 'Just let me open the door.'

It had been years since anyone had been inside, and the tiny building was in the clutch of ivy and moss. The door had swollen, and I had to heave it with my shoulder to get it open.

Once Maswe had slithered into the narrow room he collapsed on the floor and lay without moving. I knew he was alive by his rasping breath.

'Maswe – Maswe!' I called. 'Don't go to sleep.' I touched his arm. 'I'll be back in a minute.'

It was pouring now, and my clothes and hair were sodden. I ran back into the house, grabbed a blanket off my bed and raced back down the passage to the kitchen. I rooted about under the sink and found the torch and first-aid kit Seraphina kept there. A kettle was on the stove, the water boiled but no longer hot. I snatched it up, together with a cup, and tore through the backyard to the end of the garden.

'Maswe, I'm back!'

By the light from the open door behind me, I could see that he was exactly as I'd left him. Hattie had stretched herself out alongside him. At first I wanted to drag her away, but then I thought it was probably OK. She was keeping him warm. I crouched for a moment beside them. Gloomy even on a sunny day, the

51

room was now thick with darkness. I flicked on the torch.

'Jeepers!' I gasped. I could now see just how badly hurt he was. His wrists and ankles were puffed up and ringed with raw lacerations. Wherever it was exposed, Maswe's dark skin was covered with plum-purple bruises and weeping cuts. One side of his face was swollen. His left eye looked like a squashed insect. But most shocking of all was the grid of deep, straight scratches that crossed his face. They travelled down over his eyelids and across his eyebrows and nose like the outline of a game of noughts and crosses.

'Who did this to you, Maswe?' My stomach began to churn.

He needed a doctor. Urgently. He could have broken bones. Or worse. I ran the torchlight over him again. Some of his wounds looked infected. I felt a rush of blood to my ears and my heart began to pound. Who could I get to help him? He didn't want Mom or Dad or Seraphina to know. I didn't know anyone else I could trust. Maybe Gladys, Dad's black nurse. But that was no use. She'd gone off to the Transkei, hundreds of miles away, to look after her sick mother. I couldn't reach her even if I wanted to and, besides, Maswe needed help now. He was depending on me. I was on my own. I began to sweat and then shiver. I had to do something.

'Maswe – I'm going to clean you up a bit.' My fingers trembled as I opened the first-aid box.

Maswe didn't reply.

'Maswe!'

Jeepers – was he asleep or unconscious? I shook his shoulder. He groaned and flapped his hand a bit. Asleep. I loaded a bit of cotton wool with Dettol and hovered above him.

'What should I do, Hattie?'

If I started swabbing him with disinfectant, he would definitely wake up. But maybe it would be better for him to sleep for a while. He was obviously exhausted. I stuffed the cotton-wool ball into my pocket. Slowly I lowered my hand to his spangled hair and touched each water diamond one by one with my forefinger.

When Hattie growled and jerked upright I started.

'Hattie! What is it?'

She squeezed past me and darted into the garden.

'Must be Mom and Dad back.'

I draped the blanket around Maswe. I flicked the torch off, then on again, unsure whether my parents would spot the light coming from the room.

'I've got to go, Maswe. I –'

Hattie's barking jolted me into action. I pulled the door to behind me and ran back to the house.

Chapter Nine

'Darling – we're back! And come and see who else is here.'

I just had time to drag my dressing gown over my wet clothes when Mom peered round my bedroom door.

'Victoria,' she whispered, 'the Conways are here. They want to celebrate Daddy's accepting the new post. Please don't be rude.'

She looked at my wet hair. 'Were you in the shower when they rang the bell? They were on the doorstep when we arrived. Dry your hair and get dressed.'

I scowled. The Conways – that's all I needed.

'I'm going to bed,' I said.

'But it's only six o'clock! Darling, just come and say hello. Please.'

When I heard the pop of a cork and the gurgle and tinkle of liquid and glasses I hesitated outside the sitting room. I had to get back to Maswe. I did not want to celebrate. I was just about to slink away when Mom appeared, carrying a tray of savouries.

'Don't be shy, sweetie.'

I followed Mom into the room. Dr Conway and his wife were sitting on the arms of Dad's chair. Dad was broad and solid, but even he looked overpowered. Dr Conway turned his head to gulp some champagne. I watched his fish lips magnified through the base of his glass. He caught my eye.

'Ah – it's the young lady!' he exclaimed.

'Oh, Vicky – I've got something for you.' Mrs Conway got up and went to fetch something from beside the sofa. 'It's just a small thing. I spotted it in a boutique near me and thought you'd like it. Got no girlies of my own to spoil, you see!'

Then she and her husband both bore down on me, the billow of Mrs Conway's brown and purple kaftan deflating long after she'd stopped moving. Dr Conway pressed his chin into his neck. I pulled away, but not before he let out a garlicky burp.

'Now, Vicky –' Mrs Conway smiled and the light caught the marigold-coloured hairs on her upper lip – 'the next time I see you I want this filled with pictures of dishy boys.'

She held out a photograph album. On the cover was a curly-lashed cartoon girl. Heart-shaped thought bubbles were coming out of her perm.

'And who's going to be the first in the book?' Mrs

Conway asked, giving me a sharp nudge with her elbow.

I did not answer. I could see my mother miming smiles behind Mrs Conway's back, but I could only think of Maswe, lying hurt in the cold, damp room. Mrs Conway held out the album, but I didn't take it. Dad got up and strode over to my side. He touched me lightly on the top of my head.

'Thank you, Marguerite. It's a great present. Victoria's a bit under the weather at the moment. Nothing that a good night's sleep won't fix.'

He took the gift and put it in my hand. 'We all excuse you. Go to bed now, Victoria.'

'And I'll pop in on you when I check on Charlie in a little while,' Mom added.

I stomped down the passage, back to my room. Great – now I was trapped in my room while Maswe was lying in a heap outside, and they were drinking champagne.

As soon as I reached my bedroom I flung the photograph album down. What would she say if I put Maswe's photo in it? I mimicked Mrs Conway's high-pitched voice: 'Oh, Vicky – it's not a record of your servants. Why would you want to put a picture of a dirty, stinky black in your lovely, pure, white girl's album?' I paced up and down my bedroom, giving the album a kick every so often. And how dare she call me

Vicky. There was only one person I allowed to call me by a nickname.

From the sitting room, Mrs Conway's hyena laugh alternated with her husband's dull drone. I could hardly hear my parents' voices. Well, it looked like the Conways were there for a while and, not knowing when my mother might appear, I sighed and lay down on my bed.

Chapter Ten

I woke with a jerk. Apart from the usual creaks, the house was silent. Outside, I could hear the thick rush of rain and the gargling of the drains. For a moment I wondered why I was lying fully dressed on top of my bed. Of course – I'd fallen asleep waiting for the Conways to disappear. I checked my watch. Nine thirty. It was light outside. Sunday morning. I leaped off the bed and ran down the passage.

Stuck to the kitchen door was a note: 'Daddy operating – emergency. Charlie and I at Granny's. Phone if you want me to collect you. Probably back late.'

I hurtled out into the garden.

The door to what I was beginning to think of as Maswe's room was still shut. It had expanded in the rain, and I had to throw my weight against it. I stumbled into the room to find Maswe lying as I'd left him – except that now he seemed too still. Panicking, I pressed my face next to his, to check that he was breathing. Just as I'd seen Mom do with Charlie. His breath was quiet, but steady.

'Thank goodness, thank goodness,' I murmured.

And just as my mother did, I brushed my lips across the top of his head. His hair smelled of old sweat and mud, blood and vomit – a long way away from the Elizabeth Ann baby shampoo Seraphina had used to wash both my hair and his. I was suddenly embarrassed at what I'd just done and crept to the corner of the room, where Hattie was sitting. Seraphina would be in church now, probably praying for Maswe, believing him to be roaming about hundreds of miles away.

'Well, he's here, Hattie,' I mumbled into the dog's neck, 'and it's up to us to look after him.'

'Still talking . . . to that . . . mad dog . . . hey, Tori?'

The dry rasp of Maswe's voice startled me. I looked around, expecting someone else to be there. Maswe gave a parched laugh. His smile was the only recognizable part of the swollen mask that had become his face. He began to cough.

I scrabbled for the cup and lifted his head. His Adam's apple rose and fell slowly as he drank.

In the metallic morning light his sores looked more lurid. He looked like an example in one of Dad's medical textbooks, showing rare diseases in sharp colour.

'Maswe – I think I'd better clean your wounds.'

He sank back to the floor and closed his eye. Some water trickled out of the side of his mouth. I gulped back a swell of squeamishness as I dripped water from the kettle over his sores, then tipped Dettol on to some cotton-wool swabs.

I was trying not to breathe through my nose as I dabbed gingerly at his skin. He didn't flinch. I had to not think about the blood and pus I was mopping up. The pile of cotton-wool balls, smeared with yellow, red and brown, grew beside Maswe. I had to bat Hattie away from them.

'I'm sorry, Maswe – that's the best I can do.' I closed the first-aid box. I'd used up a whole bottle of disinfectant and a roll of cotton wool.

'Thank you, doctor.'

'Now – tell me what happened to you.'

He lay back on the floor. 'You sound like my mother.' His voice cracked.

'But I need to know, Maswe. Who did this to you?'

He turned his head away. 'I cannot speak of it. Your life will be in danger. Already you have done too much.'

'Rubbish, Maswe. I haven't done anything. Anyway,' I added, using the cotton-wool wrapping to gather together all the swabs, 'whoever did this to you shouldn't be allowed to get away with it.'

Maswe raised himself on to his elbow and grabbed my arm. The white of his one open eye was yellowed and bloodshot.

'You just don't get it, do you, Victoria?' He spoke slowly, his voice hoarse. 'Listen – these people are ruthless. I don't care what they do to me, but no one else must be harmed – especially not my mother.' He loosened his grip. 'I should not have come here.' He began to cough again. He drank some water. 'I am sorry, Victoria.' His tone softened. 'I did not mean to hurt you. Thank you for your help. I will leave soon.'

I could see that he had closed himself off. I crouched, without moving, as I watched him collapse into sleep again.

I'd never seen Maswe so serious. I felt a sour swirl of fear and worry. Who were the people he'd mentioned? How much more harm could they do?

I left Maswe only when Hattie began to bark. Someone was arriving. I just had time to run into the house, throw away the swabs and replace the first-aid kit in the kitchen when Mom appeared. She handed Charlie to me and put a plastic bag on to the counter. She wrinkled her nose after kissing me.

'What's that Dettol smell? Did you hurt yourself?'

'Just a small cut. What's in the bag?'

'Granny sent you some of your favourite biscuits. Crunchies, I think. Take some to school tomorrow. Doesn't Elise like them too?'

Elise. I hardly saw her. Micheline had taken her over. It felt as though she and I were travelling along parallel paths. I still missed her – the old Elise, that is. Maybe this Micheline thing was just a phase.

'Yes, she loves Granny's crunchies,' I said. So did Maswe.

I gave Charlie his bath, thinking all the time about Maswe. He'd slept most of the day. By the late afternoon he was quite a bit stronger. He'd even eaten some of the grapes and bread I'd brought him. He'd hardly said a word after his earlier outburst. I planned to slip back as soon as I could to check on him. I was worrying about getting him to the loo. How would I manage that?

Dad came back late from the hospital. It was seven o'clock when we sat down at the table. We appreciated Seraphina most when she wasn't there making everything glide into place. Mom made us clean up after ourselves so that Seraphina didn't have to deal with Sunday's mess on Monday morning. I had just taken the dirty plates to the kitchen, and was thinking about a lightning dash to Maswe's room before dessert, when the front doorbell rang. Mom answered it.

'Good evening, Mrs Dr Miller.'

I knew that coarse voice.

Chapter Eleven

It was Sergeant Kloete, and his tone was not pleasant. It sounded sort of strangled and was only just on the businesslike side of aggressive. In the kitchen I stood as still as I could, the stack of plates in my hands.

'Have you seen this man?'

There was a rustle of paper.

'But that's Maswe!' I heard my mother say.

'*Ja.* Maxwell Maswe Salwise. He is a wanted criminal and we have reason to believe he is in the area.'

'"Wanted criminal"? No, Sergeant, that can't be true.'

Dad had joined Mom at the door.

'Dr Miller.' Sergeant Kloete acknowledged him. He changed his tone. It became slightly wheedling. 'With all due respect, he is dangerous and a threat to the security of our country.'

There was another rustle of paper.

'We have a search warrant. If you please –' and his tone became curt and businesslike again – 'we would like to get on with our job. When did you last see this man?'

'About two years ago, Sergeant. He's not here. We would know if he was. Now, tell me—'

'That may be so, Doctor. I am only following orders. If you please, I will check inside. Stompie will do outside. Make the maid's room open, Doctor. Stompie will meet you there.'

I could hear Dad asking Mom where she kept the spare key to Seraphina's room. As quickly and as quietly as I could, I set down the plates I was holding and dashed out of the back door. I reached the bottom step into the yard just as Mom went into the kitchen and began rooting through the drawer of bits and bobs next to the sink. I could hear what had to be Stompie crashing his way towards the backyard from the front of the house. I had to get to Maswe. My heartbeat was pounding in my eardrums, and I could hardly breathe. I tore across the garden and slammed into the door to Maswe's room. He was awake. He looked at me with his one open eye as big as a beach ball. Without stopping, I raced over to him and hooked my hands under his arms from behind him.

'Police!' I hissed.

There wasn't time to get him out and hide him anywhere else.

'Bathroom!'

With Maswe pushing against the floor with his feet,

I heaved him into a semi-sitting position and hauled him through the bedroom and into the little bathroom. His forehead was sweat-beaded and he was breathing heavily. We both were. Next to the loo, there was an overturned iron bathtub. I leaned Maswe's back against the wall, then I lifted one side of the bath. He hunched himself up and, wincing, rolled under it. His blanket was tangled round his legs, so with one foot I shoved that in with him. The bath was heavy, and as I lowered it it slipped from my hands and clanged down on to the concrete floor.

I snatched up the cup, the torch and the remains of the grapes and raced out of the room, pulling the door tightly shut behind me.

I gulped for air as I made my way back to the house. I knew I had to slow down and calm my breathing before I reached the backyard. I needed to get back into the house without anyone noticing. I didn't want Kloete asking me questions I couldn't answer. There was clattering and crashing coming from Seraphina's room. Through the door, I caught sight of the wide back of a huge black policeman. He was swiping at Seraphina's stuff with a wooden truncheon. I felt sick. Before he turned around I leaped up the back stairs into the kitchen.

I wanted Dad to stop all this craziness. I could hear him down at the end of the passage, in one of the bedrooms. He was trying to find out from Kloete what was going on. Why was he being so polite? How dare they invade our home and trash Seraphina's room? Why couldn't he get Kloete to call off his thug?

Charlie began to wail. Mom must have gone to him, because he quietened down a bit. I stood there in the kitchen, not knowing what to do. I paced about. I thought about Maswe under the iron bath. Was he all right? Could he breathe? I hadn't even thought about that when I bundled him under it.

The oven bell began to ping. What a ridiculous tinny little sound. It took me a minute to work out what it was. Mom's apple pie was ready. Without thinking, I reached into the oven. The hot metal tin seared my fingertips and I dropped it on to the floor.

'Sergeant!' Stompie was calling from outside.

'What have you found?' Kloete shouted back. He loomed in the doorway to the kitchen. Dad was just behind him. Kloete strode across to the back door, shoving me out of the way.

'*Niks*, Sergeant – nothing.' Stompie opened his boxing-glove hands. His truncheon swung from a strap around his wrist. He was still puffing with the effort of having trashed Seraphina's room.

Good. Maybe they would go now.

'Well, search the garden!' Kloete bellowed. He trotted down the back steps, muttering, 'Stupid Kaffir.'

My stomach squeezed up like a clenched fist. Please don't let them find Maswe, I prayed. Dad came to stand next to me. He still had his napkin in his hand. His knuckles were white and I could see the pulse in the base of his neck. He was breathing quickly.

'Can't you do something, Dad?'

He put his arm around me. I could feel the rapping of his heart, and his hand shaking on my shoulder. He was just as frightened as I was. It made me feel panicky.

'Michael – what's this all about?' Mom rushed into the kitchen with Charlie squashed up against her chest. Her eyes were stretched wide.

'He wouldn't tell me,' Dad said. His voice rose in anger. 'What can they possibly want with Maswe?' He banged his fist against the kitchen counter. 'When will they stop hounding these people?'

'Have you seen what he did to Seraphina's room?' I said. 'What are we going to tell Seraphina?'

Dad shook his head. He took a deep breath. 'Let's . . . let's go back into the dining room. Just let them get on with it. When they realize there's nothing for them here they'll leave.' He ushered Mom and me out of the room.

I could hear frenzied barking from the garden. Hattie! What if they harmed her? What if she led them to Maswe? Shaking myself free from Dad, I blundered down the steps, back into the garden.

Stompie was crashing about in the summerhouse next to our pool. Kloete was prowling around the

67

garden. The rain had stopped, but it was dark. Like at the beginning of a magician's show, his torch beam lit up the house, the pool and then the pine trees that surrounded our garden. I crouched behind a bush. Hattie had stationed herself outside Maswe's room. She was getting hoarse from barking. Like a siren from some ancient myth, she was calling Kloete in. Sure enough, he strode across the lawn towards her.

'*Voetsek!* Get lost, you little mongrel!'

Kloete's glossy black boot missed her by a centimetre. Hattie began to snarl. I launched myself at her and grabbed her by the collar.

'That's right, *meisie*, get your mutt away from me before I kill it!' Kloete said. He spotted the door to Maswe's room and went to try the handle.

I gripped Hattie's collar until the metal studs dug into my palm. He turned away from the room, switched off his torch and stuffed it into his pocket. For a moment I thought he'd given up, and I sighed. Then, with a thud, he bashed his left shoulder against the door, at the same time pulling his gun out from its holster with his right hand. He stumbled into the room. The door had given way more easily than he'd expected. I held my breath.

'Stompie!' he yelled from inside the room.

Chapter Twelve

Stompie pounded across the garden and into Maswe's room. I cringed into Hattie's neck as he passed. Maswe didn't stand a chance.

Their boots rang against the concrete. They were in the bathroom. Hattie lunged towards the room, dragging me with her. I pulled her back by the collar, and we stopped just outside the entrance. I could see Kloete and Stompie, but Hattie was whining so loudly I could only just hear them.

'I smell Kaffir,' Kloete said.

Stompie's voice was muffled. He said something I couldn't quite hear. Hattie strained to move off, yelping and choking as I dragged her back.

'So what's that big fat nose for?' Kloete shouted. 'We only keep you blacks to sniff out other blacks!'

Hattie lowered her head suddenly and leaped out of my grip. She hurtled into the room and then into the bathroom, her claws scrabbling at the cement floor. Kloete was standing right next to the bath when Hattie

69

flung herself against his legs. His gun landed on the floor with a clatter. Stompie lunged at her, yanked her off Kloete and flung her against the wall.

'Leave my dog alone!' I shouted as I stormed into the room. Kloete grabbed me by the arm before I could reach Hattie. He bent over me until his eyes were level with mine. He was breathing hard. Webs of spit had collected in the corners of his mouth.

'What did I say about the bladdy dog?' He heaved hot breath over my face. Then, still clutching my arm, he stooped to scrape the gun off the floor.

'Shall we teach the *meisie* a lesson she won't forget, hey, Stompie?'

He pointed the gun at Hattie who was crouching where she'd landed.

My heart was hammering against my ribs. I swallowed loudly.

'What say you now, *meisie*? *'n Bietjie bang?* A little bit frightened, hey?'

I tore my arm away from Kloete and threw myself in front of Hattie.

'You'll have to shoot me first!' I shouted. I put my arms behind me and held on to her front paws. She was quivering.

Stompie moved towards me. He was wearing khaki shorts and his calves bulged out of his socks. His hands loomed towards my face.

'No!' I yelled. 'Leave me! Don't you dare touch me!'

Hattie growled. Kloete looked at me coldly, then jerked his head at Stompie. 'Leave it.' He slackened his grip on the gun and lowered his arm. Turning to the bath, he gave it a kick. His boot made a dull clack against the iron.

'Check under the bath, Stompie, and then we can go.'

For a second Stompie hesitated in front of me, before turning to the bath. His knees clicked as he squatted to lift the tub.

I froze. Icy prickles raced across my scalp. Any minute now and they'd have him. I had to do something. Anything. But what? Release Hattie, who was snarling? Jump on to the bath? I leaped to my feet just as Kloete's radio crackled. He turned away as he held it to his ear.

'Kloete, over. *Ja?*' Kloete stiffened his back. '*Ja, seker, Brigadier* – Yes, sure, Brigadier. Over and out.'

Digging his gun back into its holster, Kloete whirled out of the bathroom.

'Stompie – move it! They've caught someone. Could be Salwise.'

'Yes, *baas.*' He dropped the bath.

Kloete stormed past me and back out into the garden. Stompie strode off three steps behind Kloete, the back of his too-short tunic flapping. Their car doors clapped shut and the gravel ripped as they drove off.

I sat completely still for a few minutes, still clinging on to Hattie. The garden was silent, as though it too were holding its breath. My insides felt like writhing eels and my legs began to tremble. When I was sure they'd gone and weren't coming back, I let go of Hattie. She ran off into the garden.

Not a sound came from underneath the bath. I bent to lift it. It seemed much heavier than before. I'd only raised it a centimetre or two when there came a roar from beneath it.

'*Ngqundu Wako!*'

The bath rose with a jerk. Maswe was on all fours, ready to spring. I got such a fright, I almost let go.

'Maswe!' I screamed. 'It's me! Victoria. It's OK. The police've gone.'

He didn't move.

'They've gone, Maswe. They think you've been spotted somewhere else!'

Maswe's shirt was soaked and his face slick with sweat. Water ran off the inside of the bath where his breath had condensed. Slowly he inched himself out from under it, leaving a dragged, wet smudge on the concrete. I lowered the bath. Maswe crouched on the floor with his head bent, panting. Then he looked up at me.

'Are you all right, Tori? I couldn't hear what was

72

going on.' He sucked air through his teeth. 'It was that bastard Kloete, wasn't it?'

'So you know him?' I said.

Maswe gave a dry laugh. 'Oh yes – Sergeant Kloete and I, we go back a long way.' He looked at me again. I could see by the scrap of moonlight that filtered into the room that his swollen eye had opened a bit. 'You sure you are OK, Victoria?'

I nodded, but actually I wasn't so sure. I was beginning to feel cold – the kind of cold that feels like ice spreading through the core of your bones.

Wincing, Maswe spread out his limbs. He stared at the ceiling for a few minutes, then turned back to look at me. A smile flickered across his face.

'I thought they had me there,' he said.

I began to feel dizzy. I sat down on the floor and put my head between my knees. My temples were throbbing and the tremble in my legs had become an uncontrollable shake. Wrapping my arms around my shins, I tried to draw myself into a tight knot. I didn't want Maswe to see me quivering like a jelly. But it wasn't any use – I was shaking so much I was rattling.

'It's OK, Tori . . . it's OK.'

I felt Maswe's hand patting my toes. Jeepers – my feet were filthy! Immediately I scrunched them up. Maswe pulled his hand away. What if he thought I'd curled my toes because I didn't want him to touch me?

I wanted to explain that I was embarrassed about the dirt, but he'd turned away.

'Does it still work?' He was looking at the loo.

I went to pull the rusty chain. I was still shaking, so it took three yanks to get it to flush. There was a gurgle, followed by a Niagara gush.

'Yes, but the whole neighbourhood will have heard,' I said. 'You'll have to do what Anne Frank did and not flush it until the middle of the night!'

Maswe frowned. 'Anne Frank?'

'She hid from the Nazis during the Second World War. I'll lend you the book.'

Maswe had meanwhile crawled the few paces to the loo.

'I need to use the toilet. Can you help me up, please, Victoria?'

I felt a hot blush rising in my cheeks. Jeepers – I hoped he couldn't tell how embarrassed I was. I stooped to put my arm around his back and my hair swung forward and brushed against his face. He looked up at me.

'S-sorry,' I said. I scrabbled to get my hair behind my ears. He didn't say anything. It seemed like ages before he looked away. 'Um, you wanted to use the loo . . .' I said, and I tried to tuck my arm under his. He held his arm tightly against his body.

'I smell terrible,' he said.

I shook my head – too quickly, I'm sure – and kind

of shunted him on to the toilet seat. Still with his trousers on, thank goodness.

'Don't worry.' He gave a fleeting smile. 'You can leave me now, please. I can do this on my own,' he said.

'I'll come back in a few minutes.' I'd just about stopped shaking, but I was beginning to feel angry. I'd hidden him, wiped down his wounds (even though I'm really squeamish), looked after him and now protected him from Kloete. I had a right to know what he'd done.

In the backyard Seraphina's light was on, but I knew she wasn't due back until the morning. From the shuffling and low murmuring coming from the room, I realized Mom and Dad were tidying up the mess. I slipped into the laundry room. There was a stack of Dad's freshly ironed clothes on the ironing board. He and Maswe were now about the same height. I grabbed a pair of trousers and a shirt and, after a bit of hesitation, a pair of underpants. I reckoned that if he was careful with his wounds Maswe could probably sponge himself down now, so I took a plastic bucket and some soap off the shelf, together with a couple of towels. I filled the bucket with water from the garden tap just outside Maswe's room. Before I went back in, I took a deep breath. He was not going to fob me off again. He *had* to tell me what was going on.

He was crawling back into the bedroom when I reappeared. Although he was much less weak than

75

he'd been the day before, his ankles were still enormous and distorted. They obviously couldn't bear his weight yet.

'I thought you might want a wash,' I said. 'I wasn't sure if the sink taps would work in here, so I brought this bucket of water.' I set all the stuff down and went over to the sink. The taps scraped as I turned them. With a gasp, brown water dribbled out of one of them, followed by a stutter of drips. 'Looks like it's the bucket for you,' I said.

He lifted the front of his shirt up to his nose and sniffed. '*Hau!*'

I was shocked by what I saw – he'd been lean when I'd seen him that Sunday three weeks before. Now he was emaciated. His ribs grinned through his bruise-mottled skin. My stomach turned over. Maybe it wasn't such a good idea for him to wash – some of his sores were closing up, but there were still plenty that were raw.

He shifted himself so that he could lean against the wall. 'Thank you, Victoria,' he said, reaching for the bucket of water and the soap.

I needed answers, and I was not going to wait. I knelt down in front of all the stuff I'd brought in.

'I won't hand over these things,' I said, 'until you tell me exactly what is going on.' Jeepers – I sounded just like Miss van Wyk, my headmistress. All I needed to complete the picture were clasped hands and a hair-net.

Without warning, Maswe jerked forward and gripped my hand.

'You can't blackmail me with a bucket of water, Victoria!' he shouted. 'When are you going to grow up?' He flung my hand away and, leaning back against the wall, turned to look through the small window that gave on to the garden. I gasped with shock and the effort of not crying.

'Don't you think I deserve to know?' I tried to shout back, but my voice came out blurry with tears. 'I've kept you hidden, haven't told anyone that you're here – not even my father – and I'm really worried about your wounds and need his advice. I've cleaned up those wounds too, and you know how I feel about blood. And now I've guarded you against Kloete and nearly got my dog shot and I could even have been hurt by Stompie as well.'

Maswe turned his head, and I could feel the heat of the stare from his one and a half open eyes. But I wasn't finished yet.

'Whatever it is you've done has caused Kloete to come here and trash Seraphina's room and stampede through our house and frighten my mother and father and Charlie and . . . and . . . me too. Don't talk to me about growing up!' I stumbled to my feet. 'I'm sick and tired of people telling me to grow up!' I spun on my heel to head for the door and tripped on the bucket. It tipped over in my path, and I kicked it out of my way as I stormed across the garden.

Chapter Thirteen

Back in my room I lay on my bed, staring at the ceiling. My light was off and it was late, but I was still too churned up to sleep. After a while I heard Mom and Dad come back into the house and begin locking up. 'Can't you hurry up?' I muttered, willing them to go to bed. Their muffled murmuring was making me even more irritable. Mom came down the passage. I heard her open my door. She tiptoed into my room and leaned over me. Her breath was warm against my cheek.

'Darling – are you all right?'

I nodded. 'I'm OK, Mom. I just want to sleep.'

She kissed my head. 'We're just next door, if you feel upset or anything.' She tidied my sheet and tiptoed out again.

It was long past midnight when they eventually shut their bedroom door.

I kept thinking about everything that had happened that evening. My fists were clenched and my legs tensed as I lay there rigid in the dark. I felt hot then cold, then hot again. I got up and paced about my room. I gritted my teeth against the urge to roar or make some other loud noise.

Every so often, guilt leaked through into my anger: Maswe hadn't eaten for hours. He would be dehydrated. He was lying in a puddle of water. I tossed my head to get rid of these thoughts. He deserved to be uncomfortable for a while. Nobody was going to take me for granted. Or patronize me. But then I thought of how he'd looked when I'd mentioned Seraphina's room being trashed. His face had softened with child-like hurt. I knew even while I was blurting it out that I shouldn't have told him. I knew he'd worry even more about her. But the need to get at him had been too strong, and cruelly I'd ranted on. And now I felt ashamed, and cross with myself. And resentful that I felt ashamed.

I went over to the window and pressed my forehead to the cold glass. I couldn't sleep so I thought I might as well take some food to Maswe. At least I'd have that off my conscience.

The house was quiet. I crept down the passage to the kitchen and threw a chunk of bread and some cheese and fruit into a carrier bag. I also filled an old wine bottle with tap water. The torch was back where it was usually kept, and I shoved that into the bag before remembering that it was low on batteries. Well,

80

it would do for a while. The back door whined when I opened it. I waited a moment, half expecting Mom to appear. When she didn't, I trotted through the yard and into the garden. The grass was still wet from the rain, and the night air was cold. I shivered a bit in my thin cotton pyjamas. I was just going to dump the stuff. I'd be back in my warm bed in a few minutes.

Maswe lay in a heap against the wall. Hattie was curled against him. She stirred and wagged her tail lazily, then went back to sleep. Looking at Maswe lying there, I felt another surge of anger. Not caring that the crackling plastic might wake him up, I dropped the bag near his head, and set the bottle down with a clunk. 'That's it!' I muttered, and made for the door.

'Don't go!'

Maswe grabbed my ankle. With my arms flailing about, I fell sideways, hitting the floor with a flump and only just missing Maswe's legs. My left buttock was bound to have an enormous bruise. I rubbed it angrily.

'Tori – I want to speak to you.' His voice was low and a bit hoarse. 'Please stay.' He was still holding on to my ankle.

'No!' I hissed. I moved as if to stand up, but I didn't try very hard. I didn't really feel up to another scene. And there was something in his tone that made me want to listen.

'Tori,' he loosened his grip, 'I am sorry. It is right that you should know what is happening. You are

81

involved and that is my fault. I am sorry for that too. You have saved my life. That I will never forget.'

I felt awkward. He was so serious. I waved my hand to dismiss what he'd just said. 'That's OK,' I said.

'No, Tori – what you have done is a great thing. If Kloete had found me . . .' He shook his head.

'Why is Kloete after you?'

Maswe dragged himself backwards until he was sitting upright with his back against the wall. He sighed. He raised his hands and dropped them into his lap. He glanced through the window. He obviously didn't know where to begin. Seconds passed. Then he turned to look at me. I was crouching opposite him.

'Kloete thinks I am a communist. He thinks I am part of an organization plotting to blow up the South African Government.'

I wasn't expecting that. I'd thought maybe he'd fallen in with a bad crowd, that there'd been some sort of fight. 'And are you?'

'No. I am not.'

Relief washed over me. Communist plots, bombing the Government – how ridiculous. As if anyone would do that, let alone Maswe! That was movie stuff. Fifth of November and Guy Fawkes.

'There are those who are planning such acts,' Maswe said evenly.

A chill crept through me. I could feel the ungiving hardness and cold of the concrete floor through my pyjamas, but it was more than that. I'd never heard of bombing threats and communists in South Africa, yet Maswe talked calmly of these, as though they were commonplace. If it wasn't that, what was he involved in? I began to shiver.

'I am a member of Black Consciousness,' he said.

'What's that? I've never heard of it,' I said, and immediately I regretted it. I didn't want to seem a fool in front of Maswe, and I'd also had enough of people telling me to pull my head out of the clouds. I glanced at Maswe, half expecting him to say something along those lines.

Instead he laid his hand on my arm. 'Tori – you are cold.' He leaned across to the pile of washing I'd left in the room earlier. He felt the towels. He discarded one of them and took the other. 'Come here.' He patted the floor next to him.

I hesitated for a moment, unsure. Then, avoiding Hattie, I shunted myself over to sit next to him. He shook the towel open and swung it round my shoulders. As it settled around me, he gathered two corners and tied them in a knot. Where his fingers touched my face and neck, my skin began to tingle.

'Better?' he asked. He rested his hand for a moment on my shoulder.

I nodded. Couldn't breathe, never mind speak. He stretched his legs and lowered them carefully to the floor. I turned to look up at him.

'My people are slaves, Tori – slaves in our country. Our land, our culture and, worst of all, our dignity – all these have been taken from us. We have relied too long on well-meaning whites. We in the Black Consciousness movement – we believe that black people must fight for the freedom of black people. We will do everything in our power to achieve this.'

I swallowed. My voice still came out croaky. 'Even kill?'

'No, Tori. We will not kill.' He smiled. His cheeks bunched up and his front teeth flashed white in the moonlight. Jeepers – he must have thought I was such a baby. 'We do not believe in violence.'

'But if you're not a communist . . . surely when Kloete finds that out, he will leave you alone.'

'Tori, it doesn't matter whether I'm a communist or not. Kloete knows I'm involved in something. He is out to get me, no matter what.'

His tone changed. He began to speak more quickly.

'I slipped through his fingers once. He won't let that happen again. And when he gets me, he will squeeze me.'

Suddenly he took on Kloete's accent and the grating intonation of his voice.

'Names, dates, places – mostly names. He will squeeze me until I am dry. Nothing left but a mangled skin.' His arm tensed against me as he squeezed his hand into a fist and then slackened it. 'Just another stupid bladdy Kaffir communist agent threatening the safety of innocent whites.'

He paused for a moment before continuing in his own voice. 'But even if he does catch me, he will get nothing from me.' He leaned forward to touch Hattie's back. 'I will die before I betray anyone.' He spoke so softly I wasn't even sure I'd heard properly.

I didn't know what to say. I could feel the warmth of his body through the towel. I didn't want to move, ever.

We sat there in the blue-grey light. Hattie raised her head for a moment, then relaxed back into sleep with a moan. A moth flitted about. I cleared my throat.

'How did . . . ? What happened to you?'

Maswe shrugged.

'It was Kloete, right? Or Stompie?'

He sucked through his teeth. 'Others have had worse. Happens all the time, Tori.'

'What did they use to hurt you? Tell me, Maswe.'

He made a swiping gesture with his hand, as if swatting a fly.

'Fists. Pistol handles. Lead-filled hosepipes. Boots.' He stopped for a moment. 'Thumbnail.'

It took a few seconds for it to sink in. Strangely it was the thumbnail that struck me the most. I hadn't made the connection before between Kloete's thick, long, yellow nail and the grid gouged into Maswe's face. I glanced up at him. He nodded.

85

'Do you want more? No toilet, just a shared bucket. Nothing to drink out of, just the toilet bucket. No bed, just a mat full of lice and urine. No sleep.'

'You must hate Kloete,' I said. I stumbled on to the logical, next thought. 'You must hate whites,' I added almost under my breath.

Maswe shook his head. 'I hate the system. I hate the way it discriminates against us.'

His voice became stronger, more urgent. 'And every year, just when we think it cannot get any worse, the Government brings in new laws. Now they say that our children must be taught in Afrikaans.' He sucked air through his teeth again. 'Why should they learn the language of those who oppress us? How can subjects be taught in a language the teachers do not speak and the pupils do not understand?'

He banged his fist on his leg and it shook me too.

'But what can you do about it?'

'We will gather together, throughout the country, to protest against these laws.'

I had been leaning against him, so when he lurched forward I slid sideways and into the warm patch on the wall where he'd been sitting. Jeepers – how stupid must that have looked? I righted myself as quickly as I could, but he hadn't noticed anyway. He was leaning over, looking at his ankles.

'Need to get moving . . .' he muttered.

He bent his knees, drew his feet towards him and

braced his back against the wall. Then with his hands flat on the floor he began to push. As soon as I realized that he was trying to stand up I jumped up and put my arms out to steady him.

'No!' He sounded angry.

He was breathing heavily. He kept pushing against the wall behind him with the flat of his hands. There was no way his ankles were strong enough to hold him up. I couldn't bear to see him struggling, and without thinking I reached out to him again.

'No, Tori,' he said, more gently this time. 'I must do this by myself. I need to get somewhere. I need to go.'

All the while he kept pressing against the wall and pushing upward with his knees. I stood in front of him, with my hands to my face, half willing him to succeed, half wanting him not to. I didn't want him to do any more damage to himself. I didn't want him to leave.

He'd just about reached my height when his ankles gave way. I caught him in my arms as he keeled forward. We both landed on the floor, with him sprawled across me. His cheek brushed mine. I could feel the little puffs of his beard.

He swore and pulled away from me. He punched the floor and sank into a heap next to me.

'It'll take a few days until your ankles are stronger,' I said. Why did I say that? It sounded so crass. That was the last thing he wanted to hear.

87

He jerked his leg in annoyance. 'Sister, I don't have a few days. I have to pass a message to someone. I should have done it last week. People are relying on me.'

He'd called me sister. I didn't want to be his sister. I sat still for a minute. A lump like a partly chewed piece of bread stuck in my throat. I could feel tears queuing up behind my eyelids. I unknotted the towel he'd tied around me and let it drop to the floor. Hattie thumped her tail once or twice as I stood up. Maswe didn't even notice when I slipped out of the room.

Chapter Fourteen

It was already beginning to get light when I made my way back inside the house. After sitting in the dark of Maswe's room on the concrete floor and hearing, if only briefly, what had happened to him, the inside of our house seemed unreal. The patchwork quilt Granny had made me, and the pictures on my walls, looked gaudy and irrelevant.

I sat on the edge of my bed. I felt sick with disappointment. Always destined to be the small, unnoticed, drab little freak in the corner. I got off my bed and knelt in front of the mirror on the inside of my wardrobe. No wonder he'd called me 'sister'. I looked terrible: my hair straggled like dead snakes over my shoulders, and what Mom called my olive complexion just looked sallow, with dark smudges under my eyes. My pyjamas were about a hundred years old, with ducks on, for goodness sake, and three sizes too small. Elise would never let anyone see her like this – not the new Elise anyway. I had to do something to make him notice me. A blush seeped up my neck. That sounded like something out of those teenage magazines Elise loved.

I got up and staggered into the bathroom. I turned the shower on to its maximum power and let it drum on to the top of my head. By the time I walked back into my room I had a plan. Forget about the way I looked; that didn't matter. I could *do* something.

No one was awake yet when I left the house and trotted back across the garden to Maswe's room. He was on his hands and knees apparently on the way back from the bathroom when I burst through the door.

'I'll do it!' I shouted.

'What, Tori?' He smiled. I knew I still looked a mess: my hair was wet and had left swathes of damp across my school shirt, my tie was higgledy-piggledy and my laces were undone. I didn't care. I had to speak to him before Mom and Dad got up, before I went to school.

I knelt next to him. 'I'll give the person the message. I'll take it. Tell me where to go.'

I thought he was going to laugh at me or tell me to grow up and I braced myself, ready to fire up again.

He turned until he was sitting down and glanced at his ankles. Then he looked at me and nodded.

The light that morning as I walked to school stung my eyes. Everything looked too bright. I kept seeing images of Kloete raking his thumbnail through Maswe's face, and I couldn't match that with the quiet, green gardens I was passing, or their glossy parked cars.

As I approached Elise's house she came out of her gate. She didn't see me. I watched her hoist her skirt up. I wasn't sure how I felt about her. As the weeks went by there seemed to be less and less of the old Elise, and I wasn't sure whether I wanted to hang around like a faithful old dog until she returned to the way she used to be – if she ever did. Anyway, after not having slept all night I was tired and irritable, and so nervous that I felt as though a match had been lit inside my stomach. I really wasn't in the mood for any of Elise's nonsense. I waited until she'd got far enough away from me before carrying on.

'The Location.' When Maswe'd said that, I'd nearly backed out. Every time I thought of having to return there, and on my own, the burning hole in my stomach grew bigger. It was panic that kept me awake through the endless lessons. Maswe had said to go to the Location at the end of the day, just before sunset, when there would be a lot of coming and going and people would take less notice of me. I reckoned it would take me about forty-five minutes by bus from school to get to the bus stop nearest to the Location, and perhaps another quarter of an hour's walk from there to the entrance. I needed to get away from school early.

'Well, you do look rather bleak,' Miss Obers said when I asked if I could lie down in the sickroom. 'Shall I call your mother?'

'No! I mean – no, thank you. I'll be OK.'

Thankfully the sickroom was empty. I lay down on the bed for a minute in case anyone had seen me going in and came to ask questions. Once the bell for the next lesson had rung and the scuffle which followed had died down, I left the room and walked as nonchalantly as I could down the corridor and into the school grounds. I skirted the fields trying to keep to the few shadows there were.

When I reached the school gates I began to run. I reached the bus stop just as a bus drew up. This was going to be easier than I'd thought. The bus seemed empty; I chose a seat at the back and looked out of the window.

'Bunking off school, hey? And I thought you were such a goody-goody.'

It was Craig, Elise's beloved. He must just have got on the bus. He leaned over me, swirling an open can of Coca-Cola. He took a swig, then let out a loud bullfrog belch in my face. I turned away.

'Ooh, I do beg your pardon, my lady. Mind if I sit down next to you? Of course you don't.' He tossed the Coke can over his shoulder.

Craig was part of Micheline's crowd. Not very bright, and good-looking in a surfer-boy kind of way – sun-bleached hair in a pineapple cut, blue eyes (too small and deeply set, I thought) and peeling skin. I hated the way he thought all girls were after him and, if they weren't, that there was something wrong with them. He flung himself down on the seat next to me and spread his knees really wide. I squashed myself against the window, drawing my elbows as tightly to my sides as I could. I couldn't be bothered to talk to him, even though I knew there'd be some sort of price to pay.

'What's the matter, ice maiden? Oh, I see – you've never been this close to a boy before.' He laughed. 'So how does this feel, hey?'

He raised his left arm, yawned and then wound it around my shoulder, squeezing me against him.

'Leave me alone, Craig!' I hissed, and pulled away from him.

'Stop pretending you don't like it!' He drew me even closer to him, crushing my face against his chest. He stank so strongly of Old Spice I could hardly breathe. I pushed against him, but he just tightened his grip. 'You know, with a bit of effort, you could be really gorgeous. Loosen up, Victoria. Let your hair down. I bet you can't wait to tell your friends you were hugged by Craig Hofmeyer.'

I'd had enough. I was exhausted and hot, my insides

were burning up and I felt a surge of anger. How dare he taunt me and patronize me? How dare he lay his disgusting, flaking hands on me? I relaxed my body just enough to make him slacken his grasp, then with all my strength I swung my fist upward into him. I didn't know where I hit him, but it felt soft under my knuckles. I grabbed my satchel and pushed past him.

'Bloody *koelie*!' he shouted after me. 'Got more than a touch of the tar brush, haven't you?'

I strode to a seat nearer the front of the bus and sat down. The bus had stopped outside a vast Pick 'n Pay, which I recognized. It wouldn't be long until I had to get off. I willed Craig to get off before me. What if he followed me to the Location?

I could hear him moving up the bus. He was dribbling the Coke can up the aisle.

'Here you are, *koelie*!' He kicked the can at me. 'Maybe you and your Kaffir mates can make a musical instrument out of this.'

I'd heard enough of that kind of thing from Kloete. I jumped up and caught hold of his shirt.

'I hate you!' I shouted. 'Stupid and bigoted and brutish – you lot are all the same. Don't ever come near me again!'

'Or what? You'll tell Daddy?' He jerked away from me. 'Ooh, Victoria, I'm really frightened!'

I lunged at him again, but he leaped off the bus. He

94

put his nails to his mouth, pretending to be scared, then stuck his tongue out before lumbering off.

I'd never behaved like that before. Never hit out at anyone and, until last night when I'd yelled at Maswe, never really spoken my mind. I didn't recognize myself, and I didn't know if I liked what was happening. I looked out of the window for a few minutes without registering where I was. It was almost my stop.

The driver gave me a funny look when I got off the bus. This was the furthest that buses for white people went. I only vaguely remembered this area from my previous visit to the Location. The streets were deserted and dusty. There were no houses, only the abandoned industrial buildings I'd seen before. I felt another ripple of nerves and the burn in my stomach. I'd got this far; I had to go on. Maswe was depending on me. Others were depending on him.

I'd taken one of Seraphina's headscarves – it was soft and faded, the pattern hardly visible. I dug it out of my satchel and wrapped it round my head as she did, with my plait hidden down the back of my shirt. I thought it might help to camouflage me, but more than that, wearing it made me feel safe – as though she were with me. And when Craig had called me a *koelie*, it had given me a bit of courage. Maybe people wouldn't look twice at me – especially as it became dusk.

The entrance to the Location was clogged with

huge snorting, rumbling buses, each one absolutely crammed with people coming home from work. Some leaned out of the windows, shouting and waving; others swarmed around the back and sides of the buses, bundles on their heads, bags in their hands. Bitter black gusts of petrol fumes and dust billowed out and made me want to choke. I put my head down and let myself be jostled through the throng and on to one of the dirt tracks leading into the heart of the Location. Even though it was the end of the day it was still hot – hotter here than anywhere else – and sweat was gluing my shirt to my back and the headscarf to my head.

'Follow the buses to the central bus stop,' Maswe had said. It wasn't difficult – they left a churned-up trail. I spotted the soup-kitchen shed on my left. He'd said it would take about twenty minutes from there.

Chapter Fifteen

I was wrong about being able to blend in. As soon as the crowd thinned some boys spotted me. At first there were only two of them, but three others appeared. They danced around me, saying things I didn't understand, apart from 'white girl', and laughing. I couldn't tell how old they were – maybe fourteen or fifteen. Two of them were in the tattered remains of a school uniform. What should I do? Laugh as well, try to talk to them or tell them to leave me alone?

I smiled a little, but kept my head down, trying not to catch their eyes. At first I felt impatient. I just wanted to get to the bus station, find the woman, give her the message and get back. I'd told Mom I'd be at Elise's house after school that afternoon. I knew she wouldn't start worrying until about six o'clock. I had to be back before then otherwise she'd be on the phone to Elise's mother. I checked my watch. Four fifteen. I should be able to make it.

The boys had now begun to weave around and in

front of me. They were silent now, as if the rules had changed. They were closer to me as well, making it difficult for me to walk in a straight line. I kept having to stop and wait until I could dodge through them. I began to feel the drum of my heart. If this were a game, I didn't know how to play it. I kept my eyes down, watching the bare feet swap places with the canvas shoes, the bare feet, the laceless school shoes, the tyre-rubber sandals. Again and again I found myself reading the broken-up word 'Firestone' printed on the sandals. I was getting sweatier, and dizzy, and beginning to breathe more quickly. The boys weren't laughing. They were closing in. One of them, the one with the battered school shoes, made a high-pitched sound, and they all drew together, linking shoulders. I was surrounded. There was no way through.

My heart was thudding. I was panting. Sweat trick-led into my eyes. I lunged forward, hoping they'd move or that I could ram my way out. But it was like slam-ming into a wall.

'Please!' I said. 'Please let me through!' I looked straight at the boy standing in front of me. All I could see was my reflection in his plastic sunglasses. None of them moved. First Craig, now these boys. What was wrong with me? A girl was walking past. She glanced at us, then ambled over.

She was about my age, but much taller. Taller than

the boys too. Her hair stuck up in hundreds of narrow plaits. Apart from a few darns and a patch on the corner of her skirt, her uniform was neat and in good condition. Her shoes were shiny too. Her eyes skimmed over us. Taking no notice of my pleading stare, she broke into the circle, threading her arms through two of the boys'.

'*Wenza ntoni?*' she asked the boys, before jerking her chin at me.

'*Siyahavea*,' the boy with the sandals replied.

'Fun?'

The boys' faces were serious. They didn't seem to know what she wanted with them.

'*Ufanele angabi apha!*' one of them shouted. He sounded defensive.

'It is true. She should not be here. I will see what she wants.' She looked at each one in turn. Grudgingly they unlaced their arms and moved away. The boy with the sandals looked back over his shoulder.

'*Uyitombi elukhuni emhlophe!*' he said, and spat. It landed in a frothy dollop near my feet.

I turned to the girl. 'Thank you for rescuing me! I– I wasn't sure what they were going to do to me.'

She sniffed and tossed her head. 'He is right. You are a stupid white girl. You do not belong here. Go back to your deckchair in the sun.'

'I'm sorry. I just need to deliver a message to

someone. It's really important. Then I'll leave. Maybe you can help me.'

She narrowed her eyes. She didn't say anything. I stumbled on.

'This person . . . I don't know if you know her. She can be found at the bus station. Her name is Godiva.'

'You should have said this before.' She moved closer to me. 'Come quickly.' She turned down an alley and scampered along one of the less-trodden tracks behind the rows of shacks.

'Wait!' I shouted. I was having trouble keeping up. My satchel banged against my back as I trotted after her.

After about fifteen minutes of dodging potholes and abandoned oil drums and other rubbish, we emerged into a dusty clearing. The girl stopped. 'We are at the bus station.'

It didn't look like the bus station I'd imagined. There were no shelters or benches, no timetables or ticket office. Just people milling about, and children and chickens and the odd mangy dog. Buses rumbled into and out of the space, together with a few rusty cars.

'Watch out, white girl. Godiva is dangerous.'

'What do you mean . . . ?' I turned to ask the girl, but she'd already walked off and was picking her way back down the alley. I felt again the burning in my stomach and ran a few steps after her. I felt like I had when my mother had left me at school for the first time.

'Grow up, Victoria,' I muttered. How dangerous can she be? I thought of Maswe; I thought of how he'd looked that Sunday afternoon when he'd dropped out of the tree – the dimple in his cheek, which looked as though someone had dipped their finger in, just to taste. And I thought of how he looked now – criss-crossed and puffy. The burning feeling left my stomach and appeared in my heart instead. I took a deep breath, hitched up my satchel and turned back to the bus station.

Through the buses and people I made out a few bedraggled stalls selling fruit, bits of clothing and odds and ends. The largest stall, next to the sign for taxis, was the one Maswe had said I should head for. I walked towards it.

'Godiva?' I asked the woman sitting behind the stall. She smiled. There was not one tooth in her mouth. She must have been at least one hundred. Not at all dangerous. 'Godiva, I have a message—'

As I said the words I felt myself being dragged backwards by my satchel and then pushed through the doorway and into the shed behind the stall. 'Hey! Stop it! Stop pushing me!' I yelled.

After another jolt I stumbled into a small gloomy room. There was a desk and a chair. The crackle of a radio came from somewhere.

'Whoever you are, stop pushing me!' I tried to twist round, only to be pushed again – through the room, through another doorway and into a larger, lighter room at the back. I kept smelling perfume, something familiar that Elise drenched herself in.

I was so tired, and the cloying smell wasn't helping. I tripped, my legs gave way and I sank to the dirt floor. Closing my eyes, I wrapped my arms around my body to ward off any more shoving. I'd had enough. I sensed that whoever it was that had pulled and pushed me was standing behind me.

'Who are you? What do you want from Godiva?'

Chapter Sixteen

I opened my eyes. At first I couldn't make sense of the wooden shapes leaning against the walls. Boats? Jeepers! I let out a pathetic, strangled cry. They were coffins. My scalp prickled and I felt my heart begin to hammer. I was in a coffin room! A foot nudged me in my back.

'Get up!'

Staggering to my feet, I turned to look at the person who'd spoken.

Standing over me was a lean, sinuous black woman. Out of her shoes she would have been tall. In her multicoloured six-inch platforms she was a giant. She was wearing a purple trousersuit, stretched like a second skin over her curves.

'What are you doing here –' she extended a long, sparkly, purple-tipped finger and poked me in the chest – 'schoolgirl?'

She made me feel about five, but she wasn't all that old herself. Maybe twenty or twenty-five. With her huge Afro ball of a hairdo and her tight, polished skin, she looked like an advert come to life. I was mesmerized.

'You are very rude. I spoke to you. Why do you not answer?' Her voice was low, and although the purple sparkly mouth was smiling, the eyes were cold black buttons. Suddenly she scowled. 'You are far away from your big safe house. If you do not tell me what I want to know, who knows what will happen to you.' She fluttered a hand at the coffins.

'I–I need to speak to Godiva,' I stammered.

Her lips peeled back into a sneer. 'Godiva is busy. You will have to talk to me.'

Just then the old lady from behind the stall hobbled into the room. She said something, then hobbled out again. There was only one word I understood. Kloete.

'Oh no!' I said. 'Please – not Kloete.' I put my hands to my head. The young black woman looked at me.

'You – stay there!' she hissed. She ran her hands down her thighs and opened an extra button at her chest. Her breasts rose up and swelled out of her neckline. Then with a sound halfway between a hum and a sigh, she sashayed out of the coffin room.

'Sergeant Kloete. Good evening. And what can I do for you?' Her voice was breathy and caressing.

'That is a very nice costume you are wearing today.' Kloete cleared his throat. 'If I may say so.'

104

'Oh, do you think so, Sergeant? It is new, and I was not sure if the fit is good.' Her voice was silky.

Kloete cleared his throat again. 'Er, *ja*, very good. Got any information for me today? Seen anything or anyone I should know about?' He dropped his voice a little. 'Any sign of Salwise? *Jirre* – I had that bastard, but one of the new Kaffirs in the station helped him escape.' His radio roared. 'Too much interference. Reception is bad in here. Back in a minute.'

Sweat was seeping out of every one of my pores. I crept over to a coffin and crouched behind it.

'Talk to me. Or I will pass you over to Kloete.' Her perfume filled my nostrils. I hadn't heard her coming back into the room. Despite her shoes, she was surprisingly soft-footed. She pulled the coffin away from the wall and loomed over me. 'Now!'

I was stuck: Maswe had told me to talk to Godiva and no one else. How could I trust the young woman? She seemed to be very friendly with Kloete – too friendly. He'd asked about Maswe. What if she relayed what I said about Maswe to Kloete? But if I didn't tell her, she'd hand me over to him. There were too many coincidences for him not to be suspicious. He'd go back to our house in a flash. And this time he'd find Maswe.

'Sergeant Kloete . . .' she sang out.

'OK, OK,' I said. 'I have a message for Godiva from Maswe Salwise. Please, whoever you are, please don't tell Kloete.' Her face showed no feeling. She let the coffin drop back against the wall, and I winced. I could hear Kloete's footsteps again. She was back next door.

'Coffin business going well? Many deaths recently?' Kloete coughed up one of his dry laughs. 'You checking your stock, hey? Now, my girl, where were we?'

'Sergeant Kloete – it is funny you should ask about Salwise. I have just today received news about him.'

My stomach twisted and squeezed. He'd be here any minute. I had to get away. I'd noticed a door in the corner of the room. I shot out from behind the coffin and made a dash for it. The handle was a rusty nail. I couldn't get a grip, so I took off Seraphina's headscarf and wrapped it round. 'Come on! Turn!' I muttered.

'*Ja*, Sergeant, my people saw him on a bus yesterday heading for . . . where did they say? Was it East London, or Grahamstown? East London, it was, *ja*.'

What? I couldn't believe it. She hadn't told him! I stopped struggling with the door and strained to hear what Kloete was saying.

'Are you sure about that now, my girl? This is very important. The police is very interested in Salwise. Yesterday, hey? Do you know what time? I must report immediately to my colleagues in East London.' He tried to talk into his radio; his voice faded as he left the room. I heard his car rev and race off.

'And where are you going?' She was back, dragging the chair from the next room with her. Her eyes

106

glittered a little. 'Leave that door. You cannot open it.' She looked amused. 'Sit. Give me the message.'

'Are you Godiva?'

She ignored my question. From way up near the ceiling, she looked down at me with half-lidded eyes, giraffe-lashed. 'I told you to sit. Good.' She tugged my plait. 'Now – the message.'

There didn't seem any point in holding out any longer. Besides, she'd given Kloete a false trail, and that had to be a good sign. 'Maswe said to tell Godiva: protest rally on sixteenth at Location football stadium. Strike action planned for twenty-third.'

It fell out of my mouth like a stone. Then relief tinged with anxiety washed over me, followed by a tidal wave of fatigue. My eyes, my arms and my legs felt as though weights were hanging off them. I just wanted to go home. I checked my watch. Five thirty! I jerked back to life.

'I must go!'

'Not yet.' She touched my hand. 'I need to know – is Maswe safe? Is he OK?'

I looked up. Her tone was soft. There was gentleness around her eyes. She looked young. I noticed an unravelling seam in her trousersuit. She loves him. The thought drifted into my mind like a ghost and then became solid, unmovable. I knew with absolute certainty that she loved him. What if Maswe felt the same way about her? How could he not find her attractive? I felt a clawing at my heart. I was jealous.

'He's safe. He's getting stronger. I was worried about him at first, but I think with a bit more care he'll be fine.' I suppose I wanted to make her realize that I had a part to play in his safety, well – more that he was mine, really – but it came out pompous and kind of prissy. I don't know what she thought. She smiled and patted my arm.

'Thank you.'

What was she thanking me for? For looking after Maswe, or for the information? She rubbed her eye and a smear of make-up came off on her hand. She didn't seem to notice.

'I will find a way to get you home. Stay there. It is not good for you to be seen.'

She went into the room next door. I heard her radio someone, probably a taxi. She was back to the way she'd been when I'd arrived: forceful and purposeful. She strode back into the coffin room and went straight to the back door.

'Your disguise, I think,' she said, handing me Seraphina's scarf. She took a key off a hook behind a coffin. 'Temperance will be here in a few minutes. He is the only driver I trust not to talk. Too drunk to remember anything.' She unlocked the door. 'Let us hope he has not begun drinking yet.'

I glanced at her to see if she were joking. She

wasn't. She looked out into the street. The sun seemed to have been switched off. There were no street lights. The coffin room was becoming dark too.

I paced about. Five forty. I had to get going. The woman was outside. Good. I didn't think I could bear to look at her any longer. I heard a shrill whine of brakes, becoming a shriek as it drew closer.

'He is here.' The young woman poked her head through the door. 'Get in the back. You must hide yourself.' She ushered me out to the car and opened the door. She leaned in and said something to the driver, then turned to me. 'Tell Maswe –' she hesitated. 'Never mind. *Uhamba kakuhle* – Go well.' She slammed the door and strode back inside.

I crouched on the floor of the car. I had no time to brace myself. With a gnashing and wrenching of gears, Temperance swung the car round and we juddered and lurched down the dirt track. Elise's mother's driving was swanlike by comparison. What with the jolting and the alcohol fumes swirling around the car, I was glad I hadn't eaten much all day. After I'd told him where I wanted to go, he turned the radio on full blast. The station wasn't stable; it wandered between rock music, hymns and *boeremusiek*. Temperance hummed along, taking the changes in his stride.

Which was more than could be said for me. As I vibrated on the floor of the taxi, everything that had happened that day skittered through my mind. I felt

109

like I'd experienced more in the last twenty-four hours than in all the previous fifteen years of my life. If Mom had known I was travelling home in a clapped-out old Zephyr with capricious brakes driven by a drunk old man, in her own words, she'd 'have had a cadenza' – whatever that was. And to think she'd made such a fuss about my walking to and from school.

I tried to shut them out, but images of the black woman kept pushing their way into my mind. Again and again jealousy clutched at my heart. She was a woman. I was a schoolgirl, with plaits and a satchel. She was tall and glamorous and powerful. I was under-sized and scrawny and ordinary and overprotected and weak. She was black, and I was white. There was no way I could compete with her, when she'd reduced even bull-necked, racist Kloete to a jellyfish. Why wouldn't Maswe prefer her? All I had in my favour was that he was dependent on me – for the moment.

'Is your street?' Temperance was tapping me on the head. I surfaced. It took a moment for my eyes to adjust to the different surroundings. I nodded. He slammed his foot down, but we continued to coast, the brakes screaming, for a few moments. The taxi stopped centimetres away from a tree. Temperance looked very pleased with himself. Obviously one of his better halts, judging by the state of the car's bodywork.

'Thank you. Thank you, Temperance.' I leaped out and began to rummage in my satchel for my purse.

'No, missie. Present from Godiva.' He reached out and grasped my hand in both of his. '*Uhamba kakuhle.*' He grinned and pulled the door to. The car made a dry retching noise, and then roared away, scattering grit.

There was no one around. I slipped through the side gate, down the path and into our backyard. Seraphina's door was closed. I rushed into the laundry, splashed my face with cold water and dried it on a towel. My uniform looked a bit crumpled. There was nothing I could do about that. I loosened my hair and tried to saunter up the steps and into the kitchen.

'Mom – I'm back!'

'Darling, thank goodness.' Mom rushed into the kitchen. She kissed me. 'I was about to call the West-cotts to see where you were. How was school?'

'Oh . . . normal.'

'You look a bit hot and bothered. What about a swim before dinner? I'll switch on the pool lights for you.'

'No, I'll just have a quick shower.' I was halfway down the passage when I remembered what Stompie had done to Seraphina's room. I trotted back to the kitchen. 'Mom, how was Seraphina about her room, and the police looking for Maswe?'

'She took it badly. Not about her room. She didn't care about that. She's very worried about Maswe – has been for a while I think.' Mom frowned. 'She didn't want to tell us before, but the college has been

111

complaining.' She opened the fridge and took out a few onions. 'You know Seraphina – always so strong. Except now I think she's crumbling, but she won't let anyone help her. Damn –' she rummaged in the salad drawer – 'I thought I'd bought tomatoes.' She shut the fridge and began to chop the onions, wiping her eyes on her wrists. 'I told her to take the evening off. Can you just pop in and see if she's all right?'

Chapter Seventeen

When I went back into the yard Seraphina's door was ajar. Mom and Dad had done quite a good job of tidying up, but some of her stuff wasn't in the right place. The room had an unsettled look as though she were moving out, and it made me feel uneasy. Seraphina was standing with her back to me, her head bowed. The knobbly bone at the base of her neck stuck out like the top of a *knobkerrie*. Her hands hung at her sides. She was just standing there. I waited a moment. When she didn't move I whispered, 'Seraphina.' She jumped, but didn't turn.

'I am coming, Miss Joanna. In one minute I will come.'

'It's me, Seraphina, Victoria. Can I . . . I'm sorry about . . .' It would have been so easy to tell her about Maswe, and I felt the words in a roll on my tongue, ready to be unreeled. But Maswe had made me promise that I wouldn't.

113

'Oh. Victoria. Tell Miss Joanna I need to be busy. So I will make the dinner. In one minute.'

She made a quick movement with her foot, and it was only then that I noticed the photo of Maswe's father on the floor. She'd given it a kick, and when she stepped forward to pick up a fresh apron she trod on it. I knew she didn't want me looking at her, so I left the backyard and went back into the house and down the passage to my bedroom.

I sank down on to the edge of my bed and rested my head in my hands. I was exhausted, sweaty and grimy. But I'd done it. For a minute pride swelled inside me like a balloon. I couldn't wait to tell Maswe. But then I thought again about Godiva's haughty, curvaceous beauty. There was no way he wouldn't fancy her. The balloon burst. I collapsed backwards and, kicking off my shoes, I dragged my legs almost up to my chin. I felt cold, and leaden with tiredness. I thought I would close my eyes for just a few minutes, then try to see Maswe after dinner.

I woke, slick with sweat, and with a sense of foreboding. Still in my uniform, and tangled up in a nightmare I couldn't quite remember, I blinked against the light that was bleeding through the shutters. Someone must have shut them.

'Morning, my darling!' Mom padded into the room. 'Time to get up.' She pottered about collecting dirty clothes. 'You were out for the count last night. Daddy said we shouldn't wake you for dinner.' She bent to pick up my Location-mud encrusted shoes. 'I wish they'd tar the drive into your school.' She held them up and away from her. 'I'll ask Seraphina to give these a bit of a polish.' She called out as she left, 'I'll drive you to school today – I'm going that way anyway!'

I sat up, staring at nothing for a minute. Everything that had happened the day before was jumbled in my mind. It took a few seconds to separate it all out. Maswe. I hadn't spoken to him last night. I leaped out of my bed, changed into a fresh school skirt and shirt and brushed my teeth as fast as I could. Seraphina and Mom were clattering about in the kitchen so I crept out of the front door and raced across the garden.

As I neared Maswe's room I slowed down. I felt awkward. It should have been so simple.

'Oh, Victoria –'

'Oh . . . hi, Dad.'

He was in his suit, piece of toast in one hand, cup of tea in the other. Even though we'd already been in our house four years, the novelty of having a big garden hadn't worn off. He sometimes got up early to pace about like an English squire admiring his domain.

'Isn't it beautiful?' Dad waved his cup at the sky and the trees. 'Have you come out to admire the early morning too?'

'Er, no, I wanted to fetch my swimming costume from the summerhouse.' Jeepers – why did he have to be here now? I had to make him go inside. Quickly. There wasn't much time. 'Dad – wasn't that Mom calling you?'

He cocked an ear in the direction of the house. 'Didn't hear anything.' Slotting his toast into his mouth, he slid back his sleeve to look at his watch. 'It's late,' he said through the bread. He didn't notice the blob of jam that had landed on his tie. 'Better make tracks anyway. Bye, sweetie.' He kissed the top of my head. 'Have a good day at school.'

I waited a moment or two, then knocked on Maswe's door. There was no response. What a stupid thing to do. Of course he wouldn't answer. 'It's me, Victoria,' I said, pushing the door. It swung open with a sudden energy that made me stumble. 'Ow!' I hurt my knee as I landed with my usual clumsiness on the concrete. Maswe was sitting on the floor behind the door. He had pulled it open.

'Jesus, Victoria!' His voice was hoarse. 'Where the hell have you been?' He leaned towards me and grabbed my arm. 'You did not come here last night. I did not sleep.' He let go of me.

Both of his eyes were now open, the whites still yellowish, the left eye road-mapped in red. He looked exhausted.

'I–I'm sorry. I meant to, but I fell asleep.' His anger had surprised me.

'Speak to me, Victoria. Did you find Godiva? Did you pass on the information?'

I nodded, still bewildered. He leaned forward again. He took my hand between both of his and shook it a little.

'Jesus, Victoria. I have been so worried. But at least you are safe. You are safe.'

'Victoria! I'm about to leave, darling. Where are you?' It was Mom calling me. She was in the garden and coming closer.

I leaped up, pulling my hand away. 'Got to go. School.' I reached the door. 'I'll come back later.'

'Wait, Victoria! Tell me quickly. Did Godiva give you a message for me?'

I was almost out of the door. I froze. What kind of message was he hoping for? I couldn't tell from his voice. I looked over my shoulder at him. In the freckled light I couldn't read his expression.

'Tell you later. Mom's coming. Bye.' I shut the door behind me.

Mom made me take my breakfast into the car. I really didn't feel like eating.

'Don't think I can't see you pretending to eat,' she said, looking at me out of the side of her driving glasses. 'You're looking even skinnier. Dad and I are worried about you.' She rested her hand on my knee for a moment. 'Please eat, my darling.'

I nodded and bit into the now cold toast. As usual Mom drove like she was steering a vintage car, with a dignitary inside, through a cheering crowd. We saw Elise and her mother at their gate a long time before we reached their house. They were having an argument. Elise was flinging her head about. Under her chiffon tent Mrs Westcott was stamping her tiny feet.

'Let's go on, Mom.' I did not want to have to talk to Elise. Not today. 'They're having a fight.'

'I don't want to be rude. You know how vitriolic Beulah Westcott can be if she feels wronged.' She stopped the car. 'Hello! Haven't seen you for ages. How are you, Beulah?'

Mrs Westcott looked up in surprise. She put her hands to her head, trying to cover up the ranks of pink and yellow plastic rollers in her hair. 'Joanna –'

'Would you like a lift, Elise?'

Just say no – I willed her to refuse. Stay and finish your fight. I wanted to think about Maswe and Godiva without Elise to distract me. It was bad enough having to respond to Mom.

'Thanks, Auntie Joanna.' Spider-eyed from her running mascara, and sullen, she swung her satchel on to her back, only just missing her mother. Mrs Westcott lunged at Elise, her mottled face pinched into a grimace, just as Elise slammed the car door. 'Stupid old bag,' she muttered.

Mom shrugged at Mrs Westcott, who was reeling with shock. 'Well . . . see you soon, Beulah.' She fiddled with the gears and the brake and we glided off, leaving Mrs Westcott collapsed against the hedge like a melting marshmallow.

It was better than I expected, having Elise in the car. She just stared out of the window, trying to suppress her sobs. Mom didn't say a word, thank goodness. I knew Elise would have been rude, and I couldn't deal with any kind of scene.

I kept hearing Maswe's voice: 'Did Godiva give you a message for me?' I played it over and over. And just when I'd convinced myself that it was innocent, I spun it around again. And jealousy's purple-tipped claw squeezed and scratched at my heart even more fiercely than before.

When Mom stopped to let us out of the car Elise mumbled something and marched off into the school building. Mom shook her head.

'She's changed,' she said, 'and not for the better. Anyway –' she kissed me – 'have a lovely day, darling. And make sure you eat your lunch!'

I only really began to focus on school when Miss Obers took me aside after English. As deputy head-mistress, she had an office in the staff-only section of the school. She asked me to see her there during break.

I arrived a bit early so I hid in the shadows waiting for her. I emerged only when I heard her heels tapping like typewriter keys down the corridor.

It was hot in her office. The sun blazed through the floor-to-ceiling window. I began to sweat at the back of my neck, under my plait.

'I'm going to sit here, Victoria.' She pulled her chair over so that she could sit near me. We were almost knee to knee. 'I'll get straight to the point, my dear.' She picked up a pile of exercise books from her desk and, riffling through them, pulled one out and laid it open on the desk. It was mine. 'Victoria – I haven't given you a mark for the last three pieces of work you've handed in.'

I kept staring at the exercise book. I knew my work had suffered in the last few weeks.

'Victoria, I know there's something wrong.' She took my hand and pressed it. I looked up at her. Face powder had collected around the frame of her glasses. From behind them, her bright blue eyes pleaded with me. 'Something terribly wrong. Please let me help you.'

I didn't say anything. I swallowed. There were black and white and ginger cat hairs on Miss Obers's little beige cardigan. I concentrated on those to stop myself from crying.

'Victoria, my dear, you know that I wouldn't betray your confidence.' She pressed my hand again. Tears

120

swam up in my eyes. Why couldn't she be nasty, for goodness sake? I could cope with that better than kindness.

'I – I – a friend of mine . . .' I couldn't get the right words out. 'In trouble. I can't talk about it.'

Miss Obers's eyes widened. I knew immediately that she suspected that I and the 'friend' were one and the same. And that 'trouble' meant pregnancy. I took a deep breath, trying to find a way to explain without betraying Maswe. But it was too hot to think, and I just didn't have the energy. Let her think what she wanted.

'Are you sure, Victoria? Sometimes it helps to speak to someone impartial.'

I nodded and looked down again. The seconds scratched by on Miss Obers's wall clock.

'Very well, my dear.' She sighed, then tore a page out of an exercise book. She pulled the lid off her fountain pen and wrote something in her tiny handwriting. 'Here, Victoria. My telephone number and address – you can call me any time, day or night.'

'My work will improve –' I dragged a watery smile across my face – 'I promise. There's no need to mention this to my parents, is there?' The backs of my knees felt slippery against the edge of the plastic chair.

'Not if you don't want me to.' Miss Obers took a folded hanky out from under her watchstrap and dabbed at her upper lip. She stood up and went to open the door. 'Remember what I said – any time you need

121

help, I, and indeed several other members of staff –
well, we are very concerned about you, my dear.'

So many people were worried about me. Why did
that just make me feel more alone?

Chapter Eighteen

The sense of foreboding that I'd woken up with still clung to me. I tried to snatch at the shrouds of my nightmare, but they kept fluttering out of reach. That, and my conversation with Miss Obers, and not knowing how Maswe felt about Godiva made me feel closed in and irritable.

After I left Miss Obers's office, I decided to go for a walk around the school grounds. It was cooler outside than in, thank goodness. I began to feel better. When I'd stood up to leave I'd seen Miss Obers's eyes sweep across my belly. Thinking about it now made me smile.

'What's so funny, Little Miss Muffet?'

It was Micheline. She was among her worshippers, leaning against the main wall of the quadrangle. Golden-haired and golden-skinned like a storybook princess, but with the pitch- and poison-filled heart of a storybook witch.

'I think she's got a "knock, knock" joke she wants

to tell us!' Micheline leaned forward, with her arm resting on Craig's shoulder. She jerked her pointy chin at me. 'Come here. Tell us the joke so we can all smile.'

'Get lost, Micheline,' I said quietly. I knew she wanted to rile me, and I wasn't going to let her. I scanned the group gathered round her. Elise wasn't there.

'Talking about knocks – got a bit of a temper on you, haven't you? Not the polite little girlie we all thought you were, hey?'

I turned away, kept walking at the same even pace. I headed for the eucalyptus tree at the far corner of the fields.

'Don't ignore me, Victoria Miller!' she shouted. 'You want to watch your step, little girl! We're on to you.' Her voice sounded scratchy and distant, like an old record.

I just kept on walking. I had never felt so strong. My afternoon in the Location had made me feel I could do anything now. It had taken four years, but at last I knew how to deal with her. Not that this would be the end of it. I hadn't even begun to pay the price for punching Craig.

It was cool under the tree. I leaned against the trunk and took the paper Miss Obers had given me out of my pocket. The green ink she always used had smudged a bit, but I could still read what she'd written. So that was where she lived. Just down the road from Granny.

I knew exactly which one was her house. I put the paper back in my pocket and closed my eyes. And when Godiva slunk into my mind for about the hundredth time, I decided that knowing how he felt about her would be better than guessing. When I spoke to Maswe about her later on, I would face it head on. How I was going to manage that when I could feel my heart twisting and coiling with jealousy, I didn't know.

When the bell rang I made my way back to the quadrangle. This time Elise was among the group huddled around Micheline. They'd obviously just told her about my hitting Craig, because as I walked past she turned to look at me. She looked incredulous. I held her stare for a moment. She was the one to turn away first, tossing her head to dismiss me.

In the line waiting to go in there was a huge gap between me and the rest of the class. Elise had her arm wound around Craig, clutching into his waist. She was making sure everyone knew he was her property – especially me. Who knows what lies he'd told her about our exchange on the bus? He looked at me through half-lidded eyes and ran his hand through his hair. Millions of white dandruff flakes fell in drifts. It made me feel sick. How could she possibly be interested in him?

I kept away from Elise at the end of the day. I knew she'd want to confront me about Craig on the way home. I slid out of the classroom while she was scrabbling in her desk. I didn't want to walk with her, and I definitely didn't want to talk about Craig.

I got home quite quickly. Unusually, the door from the side path to the backyard was shut and I had to kick it to get it to open. It was polishing day. Seraphina had all our silver arranged on the back steps – coffee pots, teapots, serving dishes, jugs and cutlery – glittering in the sunshine. In the middle sat Seraphina. She'd put her arms around some of the pieces to guard them.

'Hi, Seraphina!'

'Oh, it's you, Victoria.' She smiled, but there was a tear halfway down her cheek.

'I'm starving!' Not having eaten much for a few days had caught up with me and, besides, I felt better now that I'd decided how to deal with Maswe's possible feelings for Godiva.

She gathered a few bits and pieces to her side so that I could get past and into the house. 'I'm coming now, now.'

'It's OK, Seraphina. I can make my own sandwich.' I was wondering whether she'd like something to eat too when I noticed her enamel plate. Her lunch sat in it, cold and hardly touched. If only I could find a way to reassure her that Maswe was safe. And not the *tsotsi* she thought he was. 'Seraphina . . .' I went over to the back door.

'I am coming, my child.' There were two scrapes as

she slid her narrow feet into her shoes, then scuffed up the steps. She put her arm around my shoulders. 'I will make you a "Seraphina Special".' She wiped her cheek on her shoulder and smiled at me again. And in that quick smile I saw Maswe so strongly that it made me want to cry. I knew it wouldn't be long before he would be strong enough to walk. And he would be leaving me behind.

I didn't eat the sandwich Seraphina made me. I took it, with some water and fruit, to Maswe's room. Mom and Charlie were out with Granny, Dad wouldn't be back for an hour or two and Seraphina was busy. I had plenty of time.

Maswe was on his feet, leaning against the wall, when I opened the door. He was shuffling, obviously painfully, back into the bedroom from the bathroom.

'Tori – look! Soon I will be able to leave. Maybe tomorrow.'

I wasn't ready for him to go. Not so soon. I was glad when he had to subside to the floor. 'Maswe, be careful.' I crouched next to him and pressed his ankles gently. 'They're still swollen.'

He shook his head. 'Protest rally is next week, Victoria. I will be there. Even if I have to crawl. Now, tell me, Victoria. Was there a message from Godiva?'

I put up one hand. 'First,' I said, 'look what I've got.' I held up the sandwich Seraphina had made.

'And, no – before you ask, Seraphina made it for *me*. If you promise not to overdo the exercises, I might even let you have a bit.'

'Tori – I have dreamed about my mother's food.' He flashed his Chiclet grin at me. 'Please.' He stretched his hand out. I knocked it away.

'Fried egg, piccalilli, tomato sauce and cheddar cheese. My – your – no, *my* favourite!' I held it up to my mouth. When he lunged to grab it I danced it away, above my head, above his head, to the side. 'You don't want any, do you, Maswe?' I put it behind my back. He leaned against me, his arm reaching behind me. I could feel the thump of his heart. We were breathing each other's breaths. Suddenly I felt awkward. He seemed a bit dazed. He drew back. Neither of us said anything for a second or two. Then I made another half-hearted joking attempt to eat the sandwich, before handing it to him.

'Only joking!' I said. 'Seraphina made it for me, but I knew you'd like it. I've gone off piccalilli anyway.'

'Don't tease me like that again, Victoria Miller!' He ate slowly. I knew this was the closest he'd been to Seraphina for ages, and that he wanted to keep the feeling going for as long as possible.

When he'd finished eating he turned to me. 'Tori – I need you to promise me something.' His eyes fixed mine. 'Tori, whatever happens to me, promise me that

128

you will look after my mother.' His voice cracked and he looked away for a moment.

'I love Seraphina too, Maswe. I always will, and I promise you that I will always take care of her.'

'Thank you, Tori. I knew that, but I wanted to hear you say it.'

I pulled at his sleeve. 'Anyway, nothing's going to happen to you.'

Maswe didn't answer. He looked into my eyes fleetingly, as if trying to believe me, but I could tell by the downturn of his mouth that he wasn't convinced. The sense of foreboding came back again. I shuddered.

'So, you met Godiva. You told her about the protest and strike?'

'Yes. Mission accomplished.' Two words. Mission accomplished. If only it had been as simple as that.

Maswe nodded slowly. Before he could ask, I said as neutrally as I could: 'Godiva didn't give me a message for you, except . . .'

'Yes?'

I still couldn't gauge his feelings. 'Except, well, she sounded like she was going to, then she changed her mind.' I decided to plough on. 'She seemed worried about you, asked if you were safe.'

'Oh, did she?' He smiled.

'She's very beautiful, isn't she?' I ventured, as breezily as I could. I had to know how he felt about her.

Maswe's face split into a huge grin. '*Ja*, she is. Very, very beautiful.'

That didn't tell me anything I didn't already know. I pressed on.

'I suppose you're in love with her.' It came out so baldly. I wished I could catch my words and stuff them back into my mouth.

Maswe looked at me. I hoped it was too dark for him to see how red I was. 'With Godiva? You must be joking, Victoria.' He laughed. 'It would be like being in love with a python.'

'A python?' I raised my eyebrows, even though I knew exactly what he meant. I was buying time. I wanted to feast on what he'd just said.

'Powerful and very, very dangerous,' he explained. I wasn't listening. 'You must be joking . . . a python' was what I kept hearing. It took a while for it to sink in. And when it did, a smile broke out across my face, a smile so wide I had to put my finger and thumb to the corners of my mouth to control it.

Maswe meantime carried on with whatever he was saying. Then he looked at me as if he were expecting an answer.

'Victoria?'

'Sorry, what did you say?'

He was silent for a moment. 'It does not matter.' He rested his chin on his hand and stared at me.

'Maswe – what . . . ? What's the matter?'

He shook his head. 'Another time, perhaps.' He patted the floor next to him. 'Tell me about yesterday, Victoria. I want you to tell me everything.'

Chapter Nineteen

'Not Kloete? I don't believe it!' Maswe clenched his fists. 'He is a vulture, circling, circling.'

'Well, Godiva knew how to deal with him. First, the sight of her in her skin-tight purple suit turned him into a gibbering fool – he kept clearing his throat when he was talking to her – like this.' I did a quick impression of Kloete. 'Then she sent him on a wild goose chase, saying you'd been spotted on a bus going to East London.'

Maswe laughed, but I could still feel the tension in him as he shifted about on the concrete floor next to me. And I felt again that curdled, swirling feeling when I thought that he would be going back out there, back within the reach of Kloete's thick yellow thumbnail, and far away from the old maid's room. And from me.

'I do not want you to go, Tori,' he said when I tailed off, 'but I am worried it is late. Someone will be wondering where you are.'

He was right. I glanced at my watch. Mom would be back soon.

'Do you – Would you still like a wash?'

He flashed another one of his grins. 'What do you think? I am not Seraphina's son for nothing!'

I fetched the bucket I'd kicked before and filled it with water from the tap outside. I dragged it back into the room and dipped a finger into it.

'Jeepers! It's cold. Shall I go and boil a kettle?'

'Thank you, Victoria, but don't worry. It has been a hot day and the air is still warm.' He swished the water with his hand. 'Very fresh!'

I heard Mom's car crunching up the drive and Hattie barking her welcome. 'I'll come back later.'

I wanted to spend as much time with him as I could. I tucked away the fact that he'd be leaving soon; from now on I would make sure that I enjoyed every minute of my remaining time with him – however short that might be. Anyway, just because he was going didn't mean I wouldn't ever see him again. At that thought I felt uplifted, light-hearted – literally, as though it wouldn't take more than a gust of wind to carry me away.

'When you come back, Tori, please bring me some paper and a pen. And an envelope too.'

I walked round to the front of the house to say hello to Mom. She was bending into the car, frantically dumping shopping bags behind her out on to the gravel like a dog in a burrow.

'Mom?'

'Oh, darling, I'm glad you've come. I'm in a tearing hurry. Can you carry these bags in to Seraphina, please? I lost track of the time completely.' She emerged, pink in the cheeks and panting a bit, with Charlie in her arms. Her bun had collapsed and her hair was tangled. '*And* I forgot it's the Dinner Dance tonight.'

She was already halfway up the front steps. 'Conways are picking us up at seven,' she said, disappearing into the house. 'Oh, Victoria . . .' She peered round the front door. 'Sorry, darling, there's another bag in the boot. Can you bring that in as well? Granny's lent me one of her dresses.'

Seven o'clock? It was already six forty. I gripped the handles of Granny's bag between my teeth. The dress inside was netted and stiff and frothed out of the top and tickled my nose. Jeepers – not one of Granny's 1950s creations. How embarrassing – it was 1975, for goodness sake! I scooped up the other bags and took them into the kitchen.

Dad appeared just then, dropping his car keys on to the counter. He ruffled the top of my head, kissed Charlie, who was now enthroned in his high chair, and grabbed an apple from the fruit bowl. 'I could eat a horse!'

'It is very late, Master,' Seraphina said. 'Miss Joanna said I must tell you the Conways will come at seven o'clock.'

'Thank you, Seraphina. I'd better hurry up and get changed then. Oh, Seraphina, do you know where my dinner jacket is?' He grimaced. 'I hate wearing the damned thing.'

'It is in your cupboard on the right-hand side. I pressed the shirt again today,' Seraphina said.

'Here, Dad,' As he left the kitchen I handed him the bag with Granny's dress in it. 'Mom needs this.'

Seraphina moved towards me and cupped her hand under my chin. 'You are looking better, my child. I have not seen you smile like this for many, many days.' She rubbed my arm, then went back to heating Charlie's food.

When the doorbell sounded I opened it without my usual dread at seeing the Conways.

'Vicky!' Mrs Conway exclaimed. 'Hello!' She was draped in peach-coloured fabric. On her head was a blonde party wig, not that different from Beulah Westcott's, high and wound round with little plaits and curls. Underneath it, her face looked like a piece of old handbag. 'Do you like my outfit? It's my goddess look!' She shrieked and waved one of her legs under its drapery.

Dr Conway puffed up the front steps. His walnut head jiggled about above the nest of shirt ruffles. 'Ah,

Victoria!' He eyes travelled over my school uniform. 'How's school, young lady?'

'Fine.' At least he'd saved me from having to answer his wife. 'I'll call my parents.'

'No need, darling.' Dad was behind me. He was still combing Brylcreem into his hair. 'How are you, Marguerite?' He stepped forward to kiss Mrs Conway's offered cheek. He slicked the comb once more through his hair, leaving a semicircle of droplets on the back of his collar. 'Joanna!' he called, looking over his shoulder to see if she was coming. 'We need to go! We're keeping Cyril and Marguerite waiting!' He gave me his comb. 'Darling, can you see where she is, please?'

'Coming, coming.' Mom appeared in a rustle and flurry of petticoats and silk. The uneven stripes of blue above her eyes and the smear of red on her lips were her attempts at make-up. She'd borrowed Granny's shoes too, and she wobbled a bit on the high heels as she came towards us – like a little girl who'd raided the dressing-up box. But she looked fresh and beautiful, and not at all frumpy. Dr Conway was staring at her.

'Bye-bye, my darlings.' She kissed Charlie, whom Seraphina had just carried through to the entrance hall, and hugged me. 'We're at the Buffalo Club. I've left the number next to the phone in case anyone needs Daddy because he's on call tonight, or in case you're worried about something or Charlie's not well. You will

136

phone me, Seraphina, if there's anything the matter, only Charlie's been a bit miserable today –'

Dad put his arm around her. 'They'll be fine, Joanna. Seraphina knows what to do.' He ushered Mom towards the door.

Mrs Conway had put on her glasses and was scrutinizing Mom's dress as Dad helped her down the steps. She hoisted up her swathes of fabric and followed them.

Dr Conway turned to me. 'You're looking more and more like your ravishing mother. Won't be long before *you're* off to dinners and dances, hey?' Before I could move away he fingered my plait, which I absolutely hated, and then pottered off down the steps. 'I must say, Michael, jolly good of you to be on call tonight.' He opened the car doors. 'I'll do this weekend. I'm sure you need a break.'

I finished my homework, Miss Obers's pleading face fixed in my mind. Charlie was a bit restless. Seraphina was singing to him in her high, clear voice, just as she did when I was little.

'Victoria, please bring me the teething gel from the bathroom cabinet,' she called as I passed on the way to the kitchen.

When I went into the room with the gel Charlie was in his cot, almost asleep. Seraphina was sitting on the floor, her arm through the bars, holding his hand.

137

'I will stay here with him for a while,' she whispered. 'Your dinner is ready. I have made you some samp and beans.'

In the kitchen, I helped myself to some of the beany, starchy stew, and put some in a bowl to take to Maswe. We both loved it. We used to fight for second helpings when we were little. I filled a bottle with water and a bag with fruit and stashed it all in a cupboard where Seraphina wouldn't look, ready to take out to him later.

I remembered about the paper and pen and envelope and went back to my room to fetch them. On the way I looked into Charlie's room. Seraphina was lying on the floor, alongside his cot, snoring gently. Mom always said she should lie down on the spare bed in Charlie's room, but she never did. I covered her with a blanket. Back in my room, I closed my shutters and arranged my bedding to make it look as though I were asleep. So Enid Blyton-ish – I smiled all the way to Maswe's room.

I had to nudge open the door with my foot as my hands were full. The bowl of samp and beans was still warm.

'Hey, Maswe – you're not going to believe what I've brought!'

Hattie groaned as she got to her feet and wagged her tail as she sniffed the food. Maswe was fast asleep. His breathing was steady, and now that his face was less puffy and it was too dark to see the grid lines, he looked more serene than I'd seen him before.

He was wearing Dad's clothes. The trousers looked really baggy and he'd mis-buttoned the shirt, and both of these things made my heart ache. I set down the stuff I'd brought on the floor near to him, and shoved Hattie outside before she could gobble up the food.

The room smelled strongly of soap. As well as washing himself, he'd scrubbed his clothes, and stretched them out on the overturned bathtub to dry.

Hattie was whining, and snuffling at the door. 'Shh, Hattie!' I hissed, hoping she could hear me from out there. I knew I'd better go before she started barking. I didn't want her to disturb Maswe. Or Seraphina.

I put Maswe's wet shirt to my face for a moment. Now that I knew how he felt about Godiva, I began to wonder how he felt about me. He'd been worried about me, I knew that. And he'd held my hand, shaken it, as if to make sure I was really safe. Well, that didn't add up to any more than the kind of feelings a brother might have. But there was that funny moment with the sandwich. I felt goose-pimply thinking about that. And then later, when he'd said something to me and I'd been so relieved to hear how he wasn't in love with Godiva that I hadn't listened . . . He'd really stared at me. What was that about? If only I hadn't been grinning like a baboon, and deaf too.

Hattie began to make a hoarse noise that I knew

would turn into a full-scale bark at any second. I put the shirt back and tiptoed as fast as I could to the door, fending Hattie off with my knee.

'Come on, Hattie!' I slipped my hand into her collar and pulled her back towards the house. 'Let's go, girl!'

Back inside, the house was quiet. Seraphina was still lying on her back, asleep on the floor. The worry crease in her forehead was still there, but she looked more peaceful than she had earlier. Her long hands lay open at her sides, Charlie's teething gel still resting in one of her palms.

Both Seraphina and Maswe were, for the moment, in my care, and it made me feel proud, and sad too. They were so close, closer perhaps in sleep – I wondered if they were dreaming about each other.

Chapter Twenty

The next day was hot, hot even at half past seven when I set off for school. The sun bored down like a yellow drill. At school I peeled my satchel off my back. My shirt was soaked. I coiled my plait up into a bun and flapped an exercise book at my neck. The classroom was empty, apart from Micheline and Craig who were hunched together at the back. I knew they were talking about me.

'Hey – Queen Victoria!' Craig shouted. 'Need a Kaffir to fan you, don't you?'

'She's so dark-skinned I bet she is one.' Micheline came over. She pointed at my back. 'She must be. She even sweats like a black!'

I just carried on transferring my books from my bag to my desk. It was still early. The first lesson hadn't yet begun. I was looking in my bag for my English home-work when Micheline plonked herself on to my desk and wound her athlete's legs round each other. She sat, chewing on her gum, watching me, a gleam in her eyes.

'Our Queen Victoria's such a good little school-girlie, isn't she, Craig?' She spoke in a lisp, then suddenly changed her tone. 'Except when she's bunking off school early and hitting people. I think Miss Obers, or better still Miss van Wyk, would like to know about that. Don't you, Craigie?' She blew an enormous bubble.

I realized my English book was already in my desk. I needed to put it in the homework basket.

'Get off my desk, Micheline,' I said. 'Now.'

She twisted her head so that her face was close to mine. She pressed her glossed lips together. 'Make me,' she said, releasing a puff of synthetic strawberry smell.

I couldn't be bothered to play her stupid little game, so I pulled a novel out of my satchel, sat down in my chair and began to read. In the meantime the classroom had filled up. I glanced over the top of my book just as Elise wandered in. She looked quizzically at Micheline, who must have mouthed something back. Elise winked at her and tapped her nose knowingly. My skin prickled, I was so irritated – more at Elise's gesture than anything else. Still parked on my desk, Micheline began to jiggle one of her crossed legs. Every time she did, the lid of the desk squeaked and her shoelace flicked me in the face. I began to simmer with anger.

'Micheline, get off that desk and go to your own seat, please. We've lots to get through today.' Miss

Obers had walked in and set a stack of books down on her table.

'Yes, Miss Obers.' Micheline smiled. 'I was just helping little Victoria.' She uncrossed her legs and leaped off the desk, patting my head as she passed. A laugh came from her cronies at the back of the class-room. I recognized Elise's recently cultivated titter.

The day grew hotter and hotter, the air stiller and stiller. At break I sat under the eucalyptus tree again. It wasn't even cool there. The air above the ground looked bendy and liquid, distorted in the heat. It was strangely quiet: no birds, no dogs, not even the whirring of locusts.

I knew it wouldn't be long now before Maswe would leave. I wondered if the weather would make any difference to his plans. If there were a storm, would he stay longer? Or would he be less identifiable in the rain? When I'd looked into his room before leaving for school that morning, he'd been on his feet again, shuffling along next to the wall. More easily than the day before, I noticed. And not holding on. He'd smiled triumphantly at me.

'I will stop being a burden to you soon, Tori. Look – I am walking!'

'Yes – but you still need to be careful. Anyway, don't talk rubbish – you're not a burden.'

'It was my mother's samp and beans that helped me! Thank you for bringing me some.'

He'd sat down for a few minutes, only to get up again and try out his walking once more. 'Soon, Tori, soon . . .'

'When do you think you will go?' I needed to prepare myself. 'You won't go without saying goodbye, will you, Maswe?'

'Don't worry, Victoria.' He'd rested his hand on my shoulder.

The rest of that school day passed with a heavy, sweat-saturated slowness. Everyone was dragging themselves about, even the teachers. When the final bell rang and the school trickled out into the unmoving air I hurried out. I saw Micheline standing next to her driver's car. She'd been waiting for me.

'Oh, there you are, Victoria. Just wanted to say – love the hair!' What did she mean? I'd worn my hair in a bun before. She whinnied with laughter and got into the car. She rolled the window down. 'Have fun – if you know what that means.'

'*Hau*, Victoria!' Seraphina called out to me from the laundry room as I crossed the backyard. 'What is that?' She came up to me, wiping her wet hands on her apron. 'Bubblegum?' She poked at something on my coiled-up plait. 'Who did this to you, my child?'

So that was what Micheline was laughing about.

'Can you get it out, Seraphina? I mean, without cutting my hair?'

She made a tutting noise. 'Come into the kitchen.'

I followed her, plucking at the stringy mass. It took half an hour of freezing with ice cubes and painstaking picking at my hair, before most of it was out. I'd walked around all day and no one had told me about it. Not even Elise. Especially not Elise.

I had a shower before going down to see Maswe. When I opened the door he was writing something on the paper I'd given him. He folded it and shoved it under his blanket.

'Tori, have you been swimming?'

'No, washing gum out of my hair.' I described Micheline and told him what she'd done.

'Stupid bitch!' he said. 'What about that little fat girl? You never talk about her.'

Elise had changed so much that for a moment I couldn't think whom he meant. 'Oh, Elise. She's changed. She's friendly with Micheline now.' I only realized just how hurt I felt about Elise when I talked about her to Maswe.

He must have sensed that, because he touched my hand and said softly, 'Don't worry, Tori. She's not good enough to be your friend.' Then he cracked a big white grin. 'I knew I did not like her when she ate up all the crunchies your Granny made. And she smells.'

145

I laughed. 'She does. She soaks herself in that disgusting perfume, and she pours eau de cologne into her hair to dry up all the grease!' I realized that Maswe was the first person I'd spoken to about Elise, and it made me feel free to be able to laugh about her.

Maswe meanwhile had stood up. He walked across to the bathroom on tender feet. But much more confidently even than that morning. Some of his old supple elasticity had come back. He went over to the clothes he'd washed and felt them.

'Still damp.' He came back and knelt on the floor opposite me. 'Victoria – listen – I will leave tomorrow.' When I tried to interrupt he put his hand up. 'I must go. There is a lot I have to do.'

'When, Maswe? When will you go?'

'I will rest my ankles another twenty-four hours. I will leave at five o'clock tomorrow evening, just before it begins to get dark.'

'Shouldn't you go in the middle of the night? Wouldn't that be safer?'

'I no longer have a pass, Tori. Kloete and his friends cruise the streets. A Kaffir in the dark is suspicious.' He smiled. 'I want to look like any black person going back to the Location at the end of the day.'

I nodded. 'Here.' I pulled my watch off my wrist. 'You can borrow this.'

'Thanks, Tori. It is so dark in here I lose track of time.' He worked the elasticated watch strap over his

146

left hand. It was my first watch, one of those sturdy metal ones with a loud tick, big numbers and glow-in-the-dark hands. It looked ridiculously dainty on Maswe's wrist.

'Do you need anything else?'

'No, thank you.' He was suddenly serious, distracted. He held the watch to the light that sifted through the tiny window. 'So, it's Wednesday today.' He tapped the watch glass, counting off days.

'Good. Tomorrow is good.' He stood up, wincing a bit as his ankles took his weight, and paced to the bathroom and back.

'I'd better go.' I opened the door. 'I'll bring you something to eat later, or tomorrow morning.'

He put his hand up, then carried on with his pacing.

Chapter Twenty-One

The next day was even stiller and hotter. Walking to school felt like wading through soup. I couldn't have bunked off, pretending to be sick – Mom would have spent the whole day fussing over me. I reminded myself that Maswe had said he would wait for me to get home before leaving. All the same, I had a gnawing feeling inside. I just wanted the day over with.

When I walked into the classroom Micheline and her gang stopped talking and turned to look at me. Someone stifled a giggle. It sounded like Elise. I knew they all wanted to see my hair, hoping that I'd had to hack some of it off. I reached into my satchel for my hairbrush and put it on my desk. With my back to them, I undid the bobble holding my hair in a plait and shook my hair loose. Slowly I brushed it out, lingering over every stroke in a way that I never usually did. I gave it one last toss before tying it up again. No one said a word, but I could feel the disappointment in the air. I should have felt triumphant – well, I did a bit –

but I was getting fed up, and I knew Micheline would only devise some new way of tormenting me.

The day moved on slowly; lesson after lesson paid out like a heavy rope. I kept checking my wrist, only to remember that I'd lent my watch to Maswe. On my way to the library at lunch break I looked through the window into the main quad. Micheline had her arm across Elise's back. Craig and the others were leaning forward, craning to hear what Elise was saying. Micheline threw back her head. I could hear her laughter through the glass. Elise broke away and trotted towards the doors into the school, her mouth curved into a sly smile.

When I returned to the classroom after lunch it looked as though my satchel had been moved. Miss Obers came in and gave instructions as soon as she reached the teacher's table. I lifted the lid of my desk. Every single one of my exercise books had gone. I checked again. Checked my satchel. Nothing apart from a few textbooks and my hairbrush. I looked behind me. Micheline, Elise and everyone else had their heads down, writing out the poem Miss Obers was dictating. I burrowed in my desk again.

'What is it, Victoria?' Miss Obers raised her voice. 'Stop rootling around and get on with your work!'

'Sorry, Miss Obers. I'm afraid I can't. All of my exercise books have disappeared. They were here before lunch.'

Miss Obers marched over to see for herself. She glanced into my satchel and flipped through the remaining books in my desk before allowing the desk lid to bang shut.

'Right! Who has taken Victoria's books?' I had never heard her speak so loudly. 'Whoever you are, you've had your fun. The joke is over.' She nudged her glasses more firmly on to her nose, then settled a stare on each person in the class, one by one. 'I'm waiting.'

I half turned in my chair. I wanted to see Elise's reaction. She stared back at Miss Obers, but looked away when she caught my eye.

'We will wait here until someone owns up. All after-noon if necessary.'

The classroom had floor-to-ceiling plate-glass win-dows. Heat poured through them, especially in the afternoon. Miss Obers took off her cardigan, draped it on the back of her chair and sat down. Someone coughed. A fly buzzed. Now and then a chair scraped on the wooden floor. Everyone looked around expec-tantly. It was half past two by the classroom clock. An hour before the end of school. I certainly wasn't going to wait beyond that. I wanted to spend as much time as possible with Maswe before he left.

There was a rap at the door and Miss van Wyk came in. She had a Pick 'n Pay carrier bag in one hand. With a tweezer action of her fingers, she pulled something wet out of it.

'Victoria Miller's exercise books have been found in the girls' toilets. And I mean *in* the toilets. If the person responsible does not own up by the end of this school day, I shall punish the entire school.' She looked at the clock. 'You have fifty-five minutes – failing which, I shall have no qualms about cancelling the Matric Dance.' She dumped the soggy book and the bag in the bin and walked out. As the door shut behind her the class exploded in uproar.

'It's Victoria's fault!' I heard someone say.

The final bell rang and of course no one had owned up. I was too hot to care. I just wanted to get out of there and home as soon as possible.

'We'll talk about your work tomorrow, Victoria,' Miss Obers said. There were sweat trickles running through her face powder. 'I will let you have copies of my notes. I'm sure the other teachers will too.'

I nodded and grabbed my now very light satchel. Elise was ahead of me. Damn. I'd hoped to get out before her. Well, what difference did it make? I wasn't scared of her. In fact, I felt a kind of power surge.

'Elise!' I shouted.

She jerked as though she would have turned round if it hadn't been me calling her. Tossing her head a little, she speeded up.

'Elise, I want to talk to you!'

She ignored me, just stomped ahead, her school bag

swinging from her hand. The sweat patch on her back grew larger and larger.

I followed her all the way back from school, only ever a few paces behind. When she reached her home she opened the gate and fumbled in her bag.

'Too frightened to face me without Micheline to protect you? Why didn't you own up today, Elise? Too scared to do that too?'

She walked up the path, unlocked the front door and back-heeled it shut behind her. I'd had enough of the plotting and the bitching and her two-facedness. And the fact that she was ignoring me now fired me up even more. I stormed up the path and rang the doorbell. A few moments later the door was opened by Agnes, the Westcott's maid. She was wiping her eyes on her apron.

'Get back here, Agnes, my girl!' I heard Beulah Westcott yell from down the passage. 'I haven't finished with you.'

'Miss Elise is in her room,' Agnes said to me. 'I'm coming, Madam,' she called to Elise's mother, and made her way back to the kitchen.

'You thieving little piece of rubbish. You stole my ruby pendant!' Mrs Westcott went on, her voice a shriek. 'I want it now. Give it back to me this minute! Then pack your bags and go, and don't ever let me see you anywhere around here again!' Her tone changed from angry to sanctimonious. 'I'm afraid my conscience won't allow me to write you a reference. But what would you blacks know about conscience?'

I was standing in the passage, listening, when Elise came out of her room.

'Victoria!' She looked startled, then furious. 'Don't tell me stupid Agnes let you in? Get out!'

I ignored her. Elise's mother had mentioned a ruby pendant, and I remembered where I'd seen it.

'Elise, tell your mother it was you who took her pendant!' I could hear Agnes pleading in the background. 'Agnes is getting into trouble for something she didn't do!'

Elise took a step closer to me. 'Shut up, Victoria, and mind your own business,' she hissed, her face pink and contracted.

'She's lost her job because of you. She's probably got small children. If you don't tell your mother, I will—'

Elise clamped her hand over my mouth and shoved me down the passage towards the front door. Her face was now puce and she was breathing quickly. I grabbed her hand and flung it aside. She brought her face right up to mine.

'What is it with you, you little *Kaffirboetie*?' She pointed her index finger at me. 'You –' she stabbed at my chest – 'are such a self-righteous prig, always going

153

on about the rights of the blacks this and the rights of the blacks that. You—'

I smacked her prodding finger away. 'At least I treat people with respect.' I could still hear Mrs Westcott ranting and raving from behind the kitchen door. 'Unlike you and your mother!'

'Don't you dare say a word against my mother!' She snatched my plait. 'Just you listen to me—'

'No, you let go of my hair and listen to me.' I tried to claw her hand off my hair. 'Let go!'

Elise wound my plait round her hand and pushed me against the wall, her face twisted into a snarl. She pinned me down with her other arm. The more I struggled the more my scalp burned.

'Elise – just get off me!'

'If you were such a Kaffir-lover you wouldn't even *have* servants. You wouldn't even live in this country.'

I tried to knee her off me, but her grip on my hair was so tight every movement hurt me more. She moved her arm so that my mouth was blocked. I kept trying to push her off, digging my hands under her arm, stamping on her feet.

'Get it right, Victoria Miller. If it weren't for whites like my parents, the blacks would have nothing. So don't talk to me about Agnes and her hundreds of children.'

Her nose was almost touching mine. Her breath

smelled of boiled eggs, and I couldn't get away from it.

'She carries home bags of our sugar and mealie meal and soap powder every week and she thinks we don't know,' Elise continued in a whisper. 'So she didn't steal that particular necklace – so what? She's stolen all sorts of other things. She would have stolen it too, if I hadn't borrowed it first. All Kaffirs are the same.'

Just as she said that I snaked my arm between us and pressed the palm of my hand into her face. At the same time, with my other hand, I reached around her and gathered a handful of her London-cut pageboy hairdo and yanked with all my strength. She flew backwards, letting go of my plait, and hit the wall behind her.

I stumbled but regained my balance before I ended up on top of Elise. I stepped over her sprawled legs. 'You and Craig and Micheline – you all deserve each other. Ignorant bigots!' I opened the front door with shaky fingers. I heard Beulah Westcott say behind me, 'What's been going on here?'

Just before I slammed the front door behind me, I yelled, 'By the way, Auntie Beulah, it wasn't Agnes who stole your necklace, it was Elise!'

I ran down the path and through the gate, my satchel pounding against my back. I'd caught sight of Elise's watch. Five to five. Without my watch I'd completely lost track of the time. Why had I bothered with her, today of all days? Maybe her watch was fast. Even if it weren't, Maswe would wait for me. He'd said he would. Wait, Maswe. Wait. Wait, I muttered, the dry heat of the day searing my throat.

Chapter Twenty-Two

I tore through the backyard, chucking my satchel down somewhere along the way. When I reached Maswe's room I launched myself against the door. My legs folded as the door flew open.

'Maswe!' I called. I could hardly draw breath. On my knees I crawled into the bathroom. 'Maswe!' He wasn't there either. 'No!' I wailed. I got to my feet. It was only then that I noticed the loo chain swinging and heard the cistern gurgling. He couldn't have left long before. I could hear Hattie barking her head off somewhere. I ran across the garden. I could see her at the far end.

Maswe was there too. Climbing over the fence.

'Maswe!' I could hardly shout, my chest heaving with dry, gasping sobs. 'Wait!'

He was already outside our front gates when I reached him, flitting between the pine trees grouped on either side. I fell against him, streaking his shirt with tears and snot and sweat.

'Tori, Tori . . .' he said. He took my hands to steady me.

'Why didn't you wait? You said you would.' I pushed against him. 'You didn't wait!'

He leaned away from me, a spark of anger in his eyes. 'You were late, Victoria! I thought you were not coming.' He collected my arms together in one of his hands, as if tidying me away. 'I have to go now.' His tone was formal. 'Thank you for your help, Victoria.' He turned.

For a split second I stood there, watching him move away from me. And then a chasm opened up inside me and I couldn't bear to see him going and I'd shouted at him and it was my fault. 'Maswe!' I screamed, and ran after him. I caught him by the shirt and he turned around. 'I'm sorry, I'm sorry,' I said, and buried my face in my hands.

'Tori.' His voice was soft. He smoothed my hair, then placed his hands on my shoulders. 'Look at me, Tori.'

I lifted my head. He was smiling, but a tear was travelling down one of the grid lines on his face. 'I'm not going away forever, you know. We'll see each other again.'

I nodded. Then a shudder rose up from my chest and I had to stop myself from crying all over again. I reached up. It felt like forever before my hands touched the sides of his face. He looked at me. Then he bent and pressed his lips to mine. So quickly and so briefly I could almost have imagined it. Immediately he straightened up. His body tensed. He frowned, looking at something behind me. There were reflections of something pink in his eyes. I looked over my shoulder. The pink was a car, moving off down the road.

He squeezed my shoulders for a second. '*Sala kakuhle* – Stay well, Tori,' he said, then turned and strode off.

'*Uhamba kakuhle*, Maswe!' I called. He didn't look back, just waved.

I watched him as he walked, watched him reach the first crossroads, and the second. Watched him until his shirt was just a small blue rectangle, disappearing round the corner. And I stood there watching him even though I couldn't see him any more.

Chapter Twenty-Three

I'd only once been on one of those fairground rides
that windmill you round and round and upside
down at the same time. I stumbled back towards our
house, and felt all over again that swooping, swirling,
curdling feeling.

When I reached the front steps I sat down. It was
dusk. The air was cool and velvety, but the steps were
still warm. I put my fingers to my lips. Had it really
happened? I wanted to bring back the feeling of his
kiss.

Hattie trotted over, her tail whisking the air. She
nosed into my skirt and threw herself on to the gravel
at my feet.

I went to kneel next to her. 'He's gone, Hattie.' I put
my face next to hers and she licked my tears. 'We will
see him again, won't we?' She wagged her tail again
and got up, and I followed her into the house.

I didn't think I could face the emptiness of Maswe's

room again, but even so, I was drawn back there later that evening. I'd left the door open when I'd rushed out earlier, and I shut it firmly behind me now as I went in. I didn't want to lose any more of Maswe's spirit to the open air. The room was dark, of course, and empty. But it was more than just empty. It seemed to hold the space that had been Maswe's.

In the bedroom he'd placed the bucket, overturned, against the wall, the soap, still wet, resting on its base. In the corner he'd stacked the blanket, the towel and Dad's clothes, all folded, the smallest items on top. Poking out of the bottom of the pile was something white. I pulled it out. It was the envelope I'd given him, sealed. I held it up to the window. Seraphina's name was written out in full in capital letters on the front. There was another sheet of paper too, folded over. My heart quickened as I made out my name on one side. I could see that there was some writing inside, but it was far too dark to read it there.

I picked up the stack of folded stuff and, burying my nose in it, breathed in as deeply as I could. Then I carried it, together with the envelope and the note to me, into the house. I stashed the letter to Seraphina in the back of my wardrobe with everything else and took his note to my armchair.

'Dear Tori, I am writing to you just a short note because I hope it will not be long before I see you again. A very short note to say thank you for every thing you have done. You have saved my life, and that is the truth. I will never forget that. Please Tori put the letter to my mother in the letter box one day or two after I have gone.' There was something crossed out, then, '*Ndiya kuthanda*. Maswe.'

Ndiya kuthanda. I knew what that meant. Seraphina said those words every day to Charlie, just as she had to Maswe and me when we were little. I love you. I read them over and over, and I felt myself spinning again into that fairground freefall, making my fingertips tingle and my heart clench.

I slept well that night, better than I had for weeks. The temperature had dropped during the night, leaving behind a slight, cool breeze the next morning. My scalp hurt when I brushed my hair and plaited it, and my skin was a bit bruised, but I felt light, clear-headed. I'd dealt with Elise. It was out in the open. I knew exactly whose side she was on, and they were welcome to her. And with Maswe's words in my mind I felt there was nothing Elise or Micheline could do that could possibly hurt me.

I went to school that Friday ready for them. I felt Elise's eyes on me a few times during the day. I thought she was looking at me strangely – sort of incredulous, and sometimes mocking – but I didn't care. Just let them start with me.

In fact, the day passed quite quickly. Miss Obers

tried again to find out who'd drowned my schoolbooks, and Miss van Wyk announced that there would be no Matric Dance (and I couldn't have cared less about that). I ignored the gathering in the playground after we were let out, ignored the shouts blaming me for the punishment. I felt separate from everyone else, as though I'd been scooped up and lifted on to another plane.

Dad was in a fantastic mood when he sauntered into the kitchen on Saturday morning.

'Morning, everyone!' He plucked Charlie from Mom's arms, kissed him loudly and passed him to me. Then he swooped Mom off her feet – 'A whole week-end off!' – and swung her round.

'Michael!' Mom laughed as she tried to recapture her flying hair. It crackled with static from Dad's dressing gown. He put her down and gave Charlie and me a hug.

'Now, who wants waffles for breakfast?' he said.

'Dad, Seraphina's not here.'

'I know that!' He cuffed me lightly on the head. 'What makes you think I can't make them?'

He did make them, and he also made an enormous mess. He'd used nearly every utensil and left batter dripping from the cupboards.

'Your father . . .' Mom sighed, but she was smiling.

163

'Don't worry, darling. I'll do it,' she said to me as I reached for a cloth. 'Why don't you go into the garden? You could do with a bit of sunshine and fresh air.'

I needed to be busy. Every time I thought of Maswe my heart lifted and I felt like I was skimming through the air. But then that soaring feeling was slashed through with fear and worry. Was he OK? Had he reached the Location safely? When would I see him again?

While Dad (and Hattie) did a bit of digging, I pushed the mower up and down the lawn. The sun wasn't as cruel as it had been; there was a slight breeze again. My arms ached and so did my back, but it felt good, and I loved the smell of petrol and fresh grass clippings. Mom brought out cold drinks and sandwiches, and we ate them under the umbrella next to the pool.

'This is the life!' Dad muttered, stretching himself out on the grass.

I went back into the house. Miss Obers had given me the stack of notes she'd promised and they were waiting for me on my desk. It was going to take days to copy them out into the new exercise books. I picked up my pen, but it was no use. I'd hidden Maswe's letter in one of Mom's old Cherry Ames books and, even though I knew what he'd written off by heart, I just had to look at it again. The paper was beginning to curl, I'd unfolded and folded it so many times. '*Ndiya kuthanda*.'

'*Ndiya kuthanda*, Maswe,' I said, and I put his letter under my left hand as I copied out the notes.

Chapter Twenty-Four

It was about four o'clock when Dad knocked on my door.

'I need a walk.' He yawned and scratched his chin. It made a sandpapery sound. 'On the beach. Do you want to come with? Mom's staying here with Charlie.'

I flexed my hand. My fingers were stiff. '*Ja*. I will. Just let me put my *tackies* on.'

Dad parked the car at the far end of the beach. We stood for a moment on the top of a dune, watching Hattie barrel down to the bottom.

'She's mad, your dog!' Dad said.

The sand stretched out like a wavy yellow ribbon with the foam for a frill. There were hardly any people this far out. Mom hated that – she was always worried we'd be attacked. But Dad and I loved it. It was much wider than the main beach, and the dry scrubland above with its scribbled-in grasses made it feel really wild. The wind always blew more fiercely there, and it

166

was soon whipping our hair and clothes. Even Hattie's floppy ears were flying around.

'Whites only – *Slegs Blankes*' a freshly painted sign warned, long before we reached the edges of the patch of beach where people – white people – herded together. Even in the late afternoon, with the sun getting weaker, the place was packed. It was the smell of Coppertone that reached you first, then the whining radios and children and the calls of the ice-cream sellers.

'Yoohoo, Dr Miller!'

'Afternoon, Doctor. Good to see you is taking the air!'

People called or waved as we passed. Dad pretended it was annoying, but I could tell by his smile that he loved being recognized.

He bought me an ice cream completely dipped in hot chocolate. I cracked the crust with my teeth and licked the soft ice cream out really slowly. When Hattie howled I tossed her a bit.

'Shall we head back, Victoria?' Dad checked his watch. 'It's quite late. Your mother will be worrying. There's a phone box down the road from where we parked. I'll call her. Tell her we're on our way.'

'And look at the sky, Dad.'

Clouds that had been so tidily swept to one side earlier were now beginning to boil. The wind had come up, even on the main beach, and people were beginning

167

to pack their stuff away. The towel was whipped off an old man struggling out of his bathing costume and into his underpants.

'Come on, Victoria.' Dad laughed and tugged my arm. 'Stop staring. Race you!'

The wind was at our backs as we made our way towards the car. As I bent to pick a few shells for Charlie, a gust scuffed the sand against my skin so that it stung. It felt like being shot with a million tiny darts.

'Made it!' I shouted as we got into the car and the wind slammed the doors shut. I laughed when I looked at Dad's hair. It was standing in stiff peaks, frosted with salt.

'I don't know what you're cackling about,' Dad said. 'You look like some sort of sea witch.' I looked in the rear-view mirror. He was right.

Dad waited in the car while I darted into the phone box to phone Mom. The door was missing and sand had blown in, but at least the phone worked.

'Yes, yes, we're fine, Mom. Just calling to say we're on our way.' Typical Mom. Worried as usual. She asked to speak to Dad. I waved at him to come to the phone. He switched off the engine and got out of the car. He gave me a rueful grin as he took the receiver.

'Joanna – what? When did they call?' Dad was

frowning. 'But it's my weekend off. Why didn't you tell them Cyril Conway's on duty?'

I could hear Mom's voice getting more and more high-pitched. Dad moved the receiver away from his ear for a moment.

'Sorry, darling. Of course you did. I'm just tired. Did you give them Cyril's son's number? He may be there.'

Mom said something, and Dad sighed.

'OK. Which police station? Starving himself, they said?' He ran his fingers through his crusty hair and sand sprayed out. 'What?' His eyebrows shot up. 'Unconscious? Right. I'm on my way. Tell them I'll be there as soon as possible.' Dad jangled the car keys and bent his head, ready to replace the receiver. 'Bye –'

Mom said something else.

'Victoria? What about Victoria?' Dad looked at me, then glanced at his watch. 'No, there's no time. I can't take her home first. It's too far and completely in the wrong direction. She'll just have to come with me. She can sit in the waiting room. Bye, darling.'

Dad slammed the phone down, and grabbed my sleeve.

'Hurry, Victoria. I've got to see a patient. Berg Street police station.'

We ran to the car. I hadn't even shut my door properly when Dad sped off.

Chapter Twenty-Five

The roads were relatively quiet and Dad drove fast, so we got to the police station in less than ten minutes. He grabbed his bag off the back seat and left me to shut the car doors.

The Berg Street station had been purpose-built a few years before, probably by the same stupid architect who designed our brutally ugly school. The front door opened straight into a waiting room, over-lit so your eyes were suddenly dazzled. There was no one behind the desk. A phone kept ringing. I sat down in one of the moulded plastic chairs and riffled through the pile of tattered magazines on the table next to me. *Fair Lady*, June 1973. *Farmers' Weekly*, September 1972. It was worse than the dentist. At least he had a fish tank to stare at. There were footsteps, metallic on the lino floor.

'Oh – Miss Miller. So you're here too.' It was Kloete. His jug ears were shiny in the bright light. He smiled. 'What an honour.'

I looked away. I could feel Kloete staring at me, and I wished I wasn't wearing the shorts I'd worn to the beach. I crossed my legs and sand dribbled out of the air holes at the side of my *tackie*. He kept on looking at me. What did he want? I snatched up the *Fair Lady* and flicked through a few pages. It settled at an article headed 'TRUST: what does it mean?' Kloete wandered over to me and stood just behind my chair so that he was looking over my shoulder. His nose was whistling, and I wished he would go.

'*Ja, meisie*,' he continued, as though we'd already been chatting for an hour. 'People has to be very, very careful who they is friendly with.' He leaned over and tapped the page with his long thumbnail. It was rimmed in reddish brown. 'And more important, *meisie*, who they is enemies of.'

'Thank you, Sergeant Kloete.' I had the feeling that his words of wisdom were supposed to have some special meaning for me, but I didn't want to hear any more. I'd been polite – surely now he would just clear off. But no. He and his whistly nostrils were still there.

'Ever been to a police station before, Miss Miller?' I shook my head.

'Police stations is very . . .' he felt for a word, 'educational places.' He moved towards the doorway. 'You must be waiting for the doctor. I'll take you to him.' He seemed to be struggling against a laugh. 'A small tour

171

on the way.' He stopped. '*Ach*, sorry. You're only about twelve. It might be too frightening for you.'

'Fifteen, actually!' I hissed. 'And of course I'm not frightened!' I jumped up and followed him out of the waiting room and down a passage. We passed offices on our left and right, and a tiny kitchen. The passage ended suddenly in a staircase going down. The first flight was lino-covered, but the second was concrete. The air began to feel cold, and the stench of damp and sweat and unflushed toilets took over from the sharp smell of cleaning chemicals.

At the bottom of the stairs was a gate. Stompie was standing guard. Kloete whispered something to him. Stompie smiled and turned his key in the lock.

'Go through.' Kloete jerked his head. 'Your father's down there. I just need to discuss a matter with Stompie here.'

I was now in a long corridor lit by flickering fluorescent tubes. They gave off a green glow. The smell grew stronger as I walked on. A black hand shot out in front of me. I nearly screamed. Then I realized Kloete had led me down to the cells. His sick idea of a joke. The person inside the cell pulled his arm back in when I passed. He was silent. The next cell was empty. I could hear Dad, but I couldn't see him. He sounded weird – his voice was loud, but I couldn't make out the words, and it was kind of raw and broken too. Angry, but more

172

than that. Like he was in shock. Something was wrong. I'd never heard him sound like that.

'Dad! Where are you?'

No answer. I turned around. 'Where's . . . ?' I shouted.

'Further on. Keep going,' Kloete called back.

I speeded up, my *tackies* squeaking on the concrete floor. I shivered. The stench of toilets began to be overlaid with something else. A cold smell – a thick, rusty, heavy, butchery stink. My throat tried to close against it, and I gagged.

'You're nearly there!' Kloete shouted. Stompie smacked his lips, making kissy noises. What was that about?

'Dad!' I shouted again.

I passed another darkened cell. Where *was* he? I was almost at the end of the corridor. On my left was the last cell. Its gate was open and the brightness of its light drew my eyes. I looked in.

I don't know how long I stood there. I only vaguely remember Dad flying out of a door opposite and grabbing me by the arm. He pulled me down the corridor towards the gate where Kloete and Stompie were standing. I'd lost all sense of where we were. I felt as though he were dragging me down a tunnel streaming with light and with a roar of rushing sound in my ears. What was Dad shouting? Why was he waving a piece

173

of paper? I tried to rip my arm away from his grasp. I needed to go back to the cell. We should be there, not here in front of Kloete and Stompie's leering faces.

'Let me go! He needs me!' I screamed. 'Do something, Daddy!'

I felt my stomach suck and heave and, as I thrashed and tore at Dad to let me go, I threw up. I threw up with such violence, it felt as though my body were turning itself inside out. Dad clung to me as I tried to push him away, and then Stompie took my other arm and forced me through the gate and up the stairs. I pulled backwards, trying to fix my feet against the rise of each step, stiffening my legs.

'Let go of me! I have to stay here!'

'Victoria – you can't. You can't!' Dad yelled.

I gave him a shove that made him loosen his hold. But then Stompie grabbed hold of me and swung me over his shoulders. I hammered my fists against his back and my feet against his belly, trying to jackknife my body free.

'*Jirre* – she's a wild thing, your daughter!' Kloete sniggered from behind us.

Stompie lumbered up the rest of the stairs. We reached the car in no time. Kloete darted ahead. He held the open car door against him as a shield, in case I lashed out at him. But he needn't have worried. Dad lifted me down from Stompie, and I just slithered to the ground.

'Victoria . . .' Dad reached for me. His voice was shaky and high-pitched. His forehead gleamed with sweat and his hand on mine was trembling. I wondered if he might be about to cry, but his mouth was pinched tight and white around his lips. 'Victoria – get into the car. Now.' I'd never seen him like that.

I tried to say something. No sound came out. Dad shook his head. He leaned down and gathered me into a heap before ladling me into the front passenger seat. The slam of my door made me jump. He got into the car and banged his door shut. He'd started the engine when Kloete tapped on the window. Dad rolled the window down about three centimetres.

'You'll bring back that form tomorrow morning. Sign it off – death by hunger strike, hey.' Kloete gave one of his dry laughs. 'You lot are all the same. The first time your . . . whatsisnames . . .' again he felt for the word, '*scruples* get in the way. But Dr Conway, *ja*, he said it would be all right. He said you also like your deckchair in the sun.' He pulled back for a second and Dad began to roll the window up. Then Kloete stuck his hand through the gap and waved his fingers. 'And, *meisie* –' he leaned forward so that his pale blue eyes were framed – 'say thank you to Mrs Westcott for me. She did South Africa a big favour. *Totsiens, Dokter!*' He banged on the roof of the car as Dad put his foot down.

*

175

We tore down the road and swerved round the next corner, the brakes shrieking as we stopped.

'How – Why . . . could they have done that? I won't – I'm not going to sign that form . . . not going to become like Cyril Conway and all the rest.' He was speaking through clenched teeth. His knuckles were white on the steering wheel. 'Not me . . . not why I became a doctor.' He reached behind him for the piece of paper I'd seen him waving. 'Won't be their accomplice!' He was breathing in gasps. 'He didn't starve himself to death. They killed him! Killed him!' He grabbed the paper, ripped it into tiny shreds and flung them out of the window.

I must have been in some sort of stupor, sitting there in the car, because I'd watched and heard Kloete and Dad as though it were all a film. 'Killed,' he'd said; 'killed' and then my mind opened up and I was back in that cell, and sagging in the corner was a heap of dead meat and it was sitting in a huge puddle of dark red blood and its head was kind of smashed in on itself and sitting comically on its shoulders but its face wasn't laughing and there was no sound except for the loud ticking from a strangely small watch and I thought I must tell Maswe when I see him next that someone else has a watch like the one I lent him and then I thought that's silly because Maswe's here and I can tell him right now and he'll think that's funny. And then Dad came in and pulled me away.

Now in the front seat of Dad's car, as I watched the paper he'd torn up whirling like confetti outside, I thought again about the blood-and-blue shirt and the canvas shoes with their laces removed, and I knew that Maswe was dead.

Chapter Twenty-Six

The house was dark when we tore up the drive. Mom must already have gone to bed. Dad stopped the car in a wave of gravel. He leaned across and put his arms around me.

'Come, darling. Let's go inside. We've got to move quickly.'

I looked at him. He didn't explain; just got out of the car, opened my door and led me up the steps to the front door. He was still trembling a bit, but he was much calmer.

'Joanna!' he shouted as soon as he'd opened the front door. 'Joanna—'

'Shh! I've only just got Charlie off to sleep.' Mom was in her nightdress and her face was covered in cold cream. She wiped her eyes on her knuckles. 'Is something the matter?' She blinked a few times before she could focus properly. 'Jesus, Michael – what's happened?' She ran to me and held my face in her hands. 'Victoria, darling – what's happened? Say something!'

178

She looked up at Dad. 'Michael, what's wrong? What happened at the police station?'

'We're leaving. We've got to get out of here. Fast.' Dad let go of my hand. 'I'll fetch the suitcases. You both need to pack.'

'What? You're not serious!' Mom looked like she was trying to coax a smile out of Dad. 'You're joking, right?'

'I've never been more serious, Joanna. We're leaving South Africa tonight.' He glanced at me. 'I'll explain later. I want to be across the border in Swaziland before daybreak, before they realize I'm not going to sign that – that death certificate. We'll catch a plane to London from there.'

'L-London? What do you mean? And what death certificate?' Mom let go of me and grabbed Dad's sleeve. 'Michael – I don't understand.'

Dad took a deep breath. He wrapped his arms round Mom and me. He began to rattle out in a kind of shorthand what had happened in the police station. My mind tuned in and out of what he was saying.

'Maswe . . . sign off . . . challenged the Security Police . . . can't stay . . .'

Mom's eyes opened wide. 'But what about my mother, and Seraphina? Oh my God, Michael – Seraphina . . .' A sob broke in her throat. 'Michael, how can we leave?' She turned and put both her hands on Dad's chest. 'Why can't we stay? What can they possibly do to you?'

I looked up at Dad. I watched his Adam's apple bob up and down before he spoke. His body began to tremble again.

'From what I've seen this evening – anything. They're capable of anything.' His voice cracked. 'I'm frightened, Joanna. For all of us.'

Then Mom began to shiver. She wrapped her arms around herself. Dad hugged both of us. 'We have to hurry, Joanna.' He took my hand and led me down the passage to my room. 'Come on, Victoria.' He hauled down the red suitcase from the top of my bookcase. 'Pack only what you really need.' He stood there for a few seconds, then went out.

I sank to my knees in front of my wardrobe. Moving very slowly, I took out the clothes Maswe had borrowed and I laid them in the bottom of the suitcase, careful not to disturb the folds that he had made. I hadn't yet posted his letter to Seraphina. I reached for the Cherry Ames book and slid the letter in next to Maswe's note to me. I put the book on top of the clothes. And then I sat down again in front of my wardrobe and stared, trying to make my eyes make sense of the stacked clothes.

Mom slipped into my room. She crouched next to me. Said nothing. We sat there until Hattie bounded in. Mom jerked as Hattie threw herself against us. She shook her head quickly and took a deep breath.

'Victoria, you haven't packed yet. Hurry.' Her knees clicked as she got up.

I swept some clothes into the suitcase and shut it. I picked it up and switched off my light.

'Are you sure you locked the back door?' Mom asked Dad as we drove away. She kept twisting to catch her last glimpse of the house. I looked in Dad's wing mirror. I felt numb.

Dad drove fast. Charlie had gone back to sleep. My window was open, and next to me Hattie's ears kept whipping my face. We were going to drop her off at Granny's house. We passed the municipal park. The trees tossed their heads in the wind like wild women. We passed the new sports complex, the shopping mall lit up for no reason, the library and Jesse James, the new steak restaurant with the sawdust on the floor. The landmarks of our suburb began to change into those of Granny's. Tessie's Tea Room, the Ritzy Cinema, OK Bazaars.

'All right! All right!' Granny shouted from behind her front door. She fumbled with the lock. 'Heard your voice through the letter box, Joanna.' She opened the

181

door, sleek in her satin pyjamas. Her eyes swept over us. 'What in hell . . . ?' she gasped.

Mom was still in her nightdress, but with an inside-out pullover on top and jeans underneath, Dad's hair was still vertical, Hattie was barking and Charlie was wailing. And I stood there, stiff with shock and covered in vomit, clutching my red suitcase.

'Let us in, Lydie,' Dad said. 'Hurry, we haven't much time.'

Granny quickly shut the front door behind us. Dad drew her into the sitting room. Mom followed, Charlie crying in her arms and Hattie scuttling at her heels. I sat down on the chair in the hall. Dad's voice was low and he was speaking quickly. I heard him say 'Maswe' a few times, and 'Seraphina'.

I opened the suitcase and took out Maswe's letter to his mother. I put it to my face. It was cool against my cheek.

'Victoria,' Granny said softly. She'd come back into the hall, her slippers whispering against the wooden floor. She bent and took my hand.

'Granny . . .' I looked up at her. Her eyes were brimful of tears. 'Please give this to Seraphina.'

She nodded, and a tear spilled out and landed on her pyjama top.

'It's a letter from . . . Maswe.' I could hardly say his name. My throat felt dry and cracked.

Granny took the letter and placed it under the little

bronze lion on the table next to me. I reached out and touched the envelope. I wanted it back.

'In the morning, Victoria, I will find Seraphina. I will tell her about Maswe, and I promise you that I will give her the letter.' She stroked my face. Her hand smelled of her favourite lavender soap.

Dad strode into the hall. 'Sorry, Lydie. We've really got to go now.'

The doorway framed Granny in her mauve pyjamas as she struggled to restrain Hattie from chasing after us.

'Will I ever see my mother again, Michael?' Mom wiped her eyes on her sleeve. Why couldn't *I* cry?

The car pulled away. With each turn of the wheels I was leaving Maswe further and further behind. Like a slide show, images of him began to click across my mind, one by one and slowly at first. Maswe dropping out of the tree. The deep dimple in his cheek. In the bush in the garden. His criss-crossed face. The flash of his smile. The images began to speed up. His swollen ankles. Trying to walk. Eating the Seraphina Special I'd brought him. My promise to look after Seraphina.

Seraphina – she was all that was left of Maswe, and I was abandoning her. I was breaking my promise to Maswe. I began to panic. Couldn't breathe, choking on air and sobs. Dad stopped at a traffic light. I grabbed my suitcase, flung the car door open and leaped out on to the tarmac. I landed on one knee and the case flew

183

out of my hand. Scrabbling to my feet, I snatched it up and began to run. Back to Granny. To get the letter. To give it to Seraphina myself. To take care of Seraphina.

Tear-blinded, crying blurry words, with the suitcase banging against my legs, I ran down the pavement.

'Victoria!' Dad caught my arm and swung me around. I hadn't even noticed him behind me. 'Darling—'

'No!' I screamed, and tried to rip myself away. 'I'm not leaving! I'm not going with you!'

Dad put both his arms around me. I clawed and bucked and thrashed until I had no strength left, and finally I slumped against him. And only then did Dad loosen his grip. Mom drove the car over to where we were. She got out and gently she unwound the suitcase from my fingers. Dad helped me back into the car.

Charlie slept. Mom sat with her head buried in her hands. Silent tears crept down Dad's cheeks. Soon we left the outer suburbs and were heading north along the unravelling motorway.

The purple mountains watched us go. We were leaving South Africa. I had no choice. But I would be back. I looked down at my feet. Maswe's blood was on my shoes.

Part Two

South Africa, January 1977

Chapter Twenty-Seven

'You is never Dr Miller's little daughter?' P.N.P. Naidoo stood behind his stall, cradling a sack of mealies. '*Jirre* . . .' He shook his head a little. 'Time flies, hey.' He smiled his streaky brown-toothed smile. 'But where did you people go? I went past your house in my truck. Mrs Miller was always wanting such a lot of fruit. But I see the house is closed up. I ring the bell, and I ring, and nobody is coming.'

'Yes, Outspan – I mean, Mr Naidoo,' I said. 'We left South Africa two years ago. But I've come back. I'm living with my grandmother now.'

'*Ja*, you can call me Outspan.' He laughed. 'I am still the orange king. Is your *ouma* wanting fruit and veg like your ma?'

'Hurry up, Pa! People's waiting,' a boy shouted.

Outspan threw the sack to his son and bent to heave a few more sacks to his feet, ready for passing on.

'Ja, tell your *ouma* I can bring to her house.' He

pulled a handkerchief out of his pocket and wiped his shiny head.

'Thanks, Outspan,' I said.

Mom had often taken me to this market when Outspan hadn't called round for a while. Even though it was still quite early, it was crowded and hot, and the heat made the smells of pawpaw, onions, sweat, petrol and dust even stronger. People pushed and shoved. Wheelbarrows and trolleys piled with sacks of potatoes nudged the back of my legs. There was the usual shouting and calling and whistling. I felt happy to be back.

I took my fruit and paid Outspan's son. As I bent to put my purse back in my bag, just out of the corner of my eye I spotted a pair of large hands, a black person's hands, long nails sparkly blue, reaching for a sack of yellow mealies. I hadn't seen nails like that since . . . I stopped for a moment. Then I whipped round. The owner of the blue nails had gone.

'Outspan – which way did she go? You know, the woman with the long nails?' I had to wait for him to finish mopping his head.

'I think she went there – there by Viljoen's Bananas,' he said. He was smiling dreamily; it had to have been her.

I don't know how I hadn't spotted her before. Taller than most people anyway, she'd swept her hair into a towering headdress. It was made of multicoloured scarves; two or three of the ends snaked round her neck and down her back.

'Sorry . . . sorry . . .' I shadowed and dodged through the crowds. She was a link with Maswe, and I just had to catch her up. She was walking deceptively fast. The stalls became sparse until they petered out into battered tables or upturned crates, and then just heaps of discarded fruit. She stepped past the women picking over the bruised produce and moved towards a tumbledown warehouse. She did not look back once, but I was sure she knew I was behind her.

The door to the warehouse whined as she nudged it open with her foot. Some flustered pigeons flew out. I followed her down a passage strewn with rubbish and splashed with bird droppings and into a tiny room. She stood with her back to the window, her arms crossed. I couldn't see her features clearly.

'What do you want, white girl?' Her voice was hard.

'*Unjani*, Godiva?' I asked. 'How are you?'

She didn't reply.

'You are very rude. I spoke to you. Why didn't you answer?' I wondered if she recognized her own words.

'*Ufuna ntoni?* I said, what do you want, white girl?'

It was only when she said those words that it came to me – Maswe had trusted her. She'd have contacts, and not just within Black Consciousness.

'I need your help,' I said.

She clicked her tongue dismissively. 'You ran away.'

189

'My father refused to do what the Security Police wanted. So we left South Africa.'

'So why did you come back? Missing your *braaivleis* by the pool, hey?'

I ignored that. She couldn't intimidate me now.

There had not been a day, an hour even, during the two years I'd spent in London when I hadn't thought about Maswe. And strangely, thousands of kilometres away from South Africa, in London's gauzy light, I had begun to believe that he was still alive. Loping in his loose-limbed way, his scars miraculously healed and his dimple restored – out of reach, but alive.

It was only when I stepped off the plane, and the heat rose from the earth and warmed my legs, that I knew with a renewed sense of finality that he was dead. And it was then that the mental slide show began again. Round and round the images went, each one clicking into place in their unstoppable sequence, and lingering always at the final shot, the grand finale – Maswe's sagging, pulped body, with the watch on his wrist ticking madly. And every time I felt again the rushing, spinning nausea of that night in the police station.

Except now, swirling through it all was guilt – guilt, with all its corroding poison. If I hadn't chased after Elise, if I hadn't had that fight with her, if I hadn't been late, if I hadn't stopped Maswe in the road, then Beulah Westcott would never have come looking for

190

me, would never have seen me and Maswe, would never have reported it to Kloete. And my thoughts twisted and churned to the inevitable conclusion: it was I who had killed Maswe.

Godiva shifted in front of me. The onions in her string bag rustled.

'I want to join Umkhonto we Sizwe,' I said. It was as if that wish had just taken form with Godiva standing in front of me. Mazwe had been part of a consciousness-raising group. But Umkhonto was more extreme. 'Spear of the Nation' – that's what Umkhonto we Sizwe, MK, meant. I liked that sense of power. I wanted to be part of it. It felt as though that was what I *had* to do now that I was back in South Africa. 'I want to join MK. I know you know people.'

'MK, hey?' She leaned towards me. 'And what makes you think MK wants you?'

'I don't need to argue my case to you,' I said.

'Then I do not need to stay here.' Gathering up a stray scarf end and flinging it around her neck, she moved towards the door. She jostled me as she pushed past.

'Maswe was murdered,' I said to her back. It made my chest tighten and my throat close up to say those words. 'I saw . . . him.'

Godiva stopped. She whirled around, her mouth somehow collapsed. She tried to catch her breath. 'Seraphina would not speak about it. But people said it

191

was a hunger strike.' She reached behind to steady herself. Her fingernails clattered against the door frame. 'They said it was a hunger strike,' she repeated.

I smelled again the raw stench of slaughter.

'I need to fight,' I said.

Godiva straightened up. She was still breathing quickly. She stepped closer to me. 'It is Abel Nkosana you have to convince.' She gave a dry laugh. 'It will not be easy, white girl.' She turned to go.

'Wait, Godiva. How – where – will I find him?'

'The main beach. He sells ice cream to people like you.' She looked over her shoulder. 'You must pretend to be choosing an ice cream. You do not know who may be watching.'

I shivered.

'And wait ten minutes after I have gone before you leave this building. Do not be careless, white girl.'

Chapter Twenty-Eight

The next day was hot. There would be loads of people on the beach. Not too many, I hoped. I hated crowds, and I didn't want anyone to overhear my conversation with Abel Nkosana – if I ever managed to find him. Sometimes the beach got so packed you'd be lucky not to get someone's sand-encrusted foot in your ice cream.

'You must take this, Victoria.' Seraphina was holding Granny's old beach umbrella. We were outside Granny's house, on the short driveway where she always left her car. 'The sun is very strong today. Your skin is not yet used to it.'

'OK, I will. Thanks, Seraphina,' I said, and hugged her. She put her arms around me. Her skin felt papery. She was even thinner now. Like a dried-out leaf, I thought as I took the umbrella from her, and it made me want to cry.

'I will tell Miss Lydie when she comes back. She will be happy you are getting some fresh air.' She watched me stuff my beach bag and the umbrella in the back of Granny's car. '*Hau!* I do not like to see you driving. You are too young, my child.' She frowned. 'It is not safe.'

'Don't worry. I'll be fine. I passed my test in London, Seraphina. If I can drive there, I can drive anywhere.'

Her long hands hanging at her sides always looked so empty now.

'Go carefully, Victoria. I will expect you for lunch.' She stood on the pavement, Hattie at her feet, watching me drive off, and I knew that if she could she would stay in exactly the same spot until I came back.

I found a parking space only a few minutes' walk away from the main beach. That was a good omen. I opened the car door; the seaside sounds were suddenly switched on: the roar of the sea, mixed up with the screams of children and seagulls, people shouting, announcements over the tannoy, and whining radios. I'd forgotten all that.

The sand was already hot under my feet as I picked my way to the edge of the beach, near a heap of rocks. I put up the umbrella and laid my towel out. In London, Dad had invited some people round who'd been involved with MK. Submit or fight, that had been their choice. And they had chosen not to submit. I knew MK sabotaged power lines and bombed police stations. And I knew that it was not about killing people. All the same, I felt a thrill of nerves at the thought of meeting Abel Nkosana – someone the police would definitely call a terrorist.

Keeping my sunglasses on, I scanned the strip of beach just where the waves broke. The ice-cream sellers used to stroll along there, looking out to the crowds on the beach, waiting to be called over. No one yet – just the usual shrieking people. I pulled my novel out of my bag and opened it. The lines kept sliding into each other and the words just wouldn't make sense. Again and again I looked over the top of the book. Still no ice-cream seller.

It was getting hotter, even under the shade of Granny's umbrella. I thought it might be cooler along the water's edge so I left the umbrella, slung my beach bag over my shoulder and wandered down. I remembered Godiva's warning. It was hard not to look as though I were watching out for someone. Stepping through the foam, I walked from one end of the beach to the other, then back again. I kept checking the bobbing mass of people. There were a few young boys among them, hiring out deckchairs, and a woman renting umbrellas, but not a single ice-cream seller.

Even with the breeze coming off the waves, it was hot. Sweat was trickling down my back. I began to feel irritable. I decided to walk along the water's edge one more time before heading back. I was hungry. Seraphina would start worrying soon.

'Rockets, Eskimo Pies, we have, Icy Oranges, and Lekkerliks also. Would Miss like an ice cream to cool herself down, hey?'

I swung round. An old black man was standing behind me. His skin was really dark, while the hair that grew like lichen over his head and round his chin was white. He carried the ice-cream cooler box under his arm like a knight carrying his helmet. A couple of children ran over to him. I waited until they'd chosen their ice creams and counted their coins into his open hand.

He looked up at me. Behind his huge, high cheekbones his eyes were small and creased, but the look in them was sharp.

'Abel Nkosana?' I asked as soon as the children had gone.

'*Ja*, Miss Miller.'

I don't know why I was so surprised that he knew my name. Godiva must have warned him about me. But it took me a second or two before I could think of what I was going to say.

'I have heard you want to join us,' he said, while kneeling on the sand and opening the flaps on the cooler box. 'Eskimo Pie, twenty-five cents.' He looked up at me. 'We know about you. We have heard from our people in London. We know about your father.' He held out the ice cream.

'There's so much I can do,' I said, digging wildly in

my bag for my purse. 'I'm not frightened. I'll go anywhere. I'll do anything MK needs me to do. I . . .'

He took my free hand and held it just for a moment
in both of his. His voice was low and he spoke quickly.
'Victoria – the police are watching, watching you. Even
today they are here. It is not safe for MK.' He shook
his head. '*You* are not safe for MK.' He closed the
cooler box and flicked the catches.

'But – but I want to fight.' I could feel tears filling
my eyes. 'I need to. Please, Mr Nkosana.'

He didn't say anything. Gathering up the box, he
got up from the sand and turned away from me. 'Ice
creams. *Roomys*,' he called.

'No!' I ran a few paces after him. How could he just
turn me down like that? 'No, please – listen to me!'

He didn't look back. 'Eskimo Pie, we have, Rockets,' he carried on calling as he made his way further
up the beach. 'Lekkerliks, Wafers, Chocomints.'

I stopped where I was and scuffed at the wet sand
with my bare feet. I'd been so sure MK would accept
me – more than that, I thought they'd welcome me. He
said he'd heard of Dad, his people in London had
spoken of him. And still they didn't want me. I looked
again at the teeming beach, now shimmering in the
midday sun. How could he know that there was someone out there, among all those people, watching me? I
couldn't even see *him* now. I kicked at the sand again.

197

I felt hot and cross and, more than anything else, I felt helpless.

I turned back to the sea. I didn't notice the waves teasing me with their spray or the ice cream melting in its wrapper until my clothes were soaked and my arm was covered with sticky chocolate. I let some sea water wash over my arm and, licking what was left of my ice cream, I went back to my towel.

I packed up my stuff and yanked Granny's umbrella out of the sand. I just wanted to get away quickly. But the beach was tightly packed now and it was almost impossible not to spear someone as I shuffled past the frying bodies.

When I eventually got to the car it was baking inside; the car seat was blisteringly hot and it burned the backs of my legs. I was coated in sand, like a piece of fried chicken, and my hair was stuck to my head with sweat. Someone had parked me in, and by the time I'd manoeuvred the car backwards and forwards about three hundred times I was in a fury. There was a dark blue car idling across the street, waiting for my space, and that didn't help either. I tried to wind down my window. I needed air – even hot, petrol-polluted air. Damn. The window got stuck halfway. I pressed the glass down with my palm, trying to force it open.

At the next lights I was just checking my face for sunburn when I spotted the dark blue car again, a couple of cars behind me. 'That's odd,' I muttered. 'I thought it was waiting for my space.' I noticed it again when I turned off the main road and on to one of the quiet suburban avenues near Granny's house. It kept the same pace as me as I turned corners and stopped at crossroads.

And then my blood chilled. Of course. I was being followed. I remembered what Abel Nkosana had said. 'They are watching, watching . . .'

My heart began to drum against my chest. I checked my mirror. Still there. I speeded up. I slowed to a tortoise pace. Speeded up again. I drove past Granny's house and back to the main road. He stuck with me. There was no doubt about it.

When I parked the car on Granny's drive he stopped across the road. I could hardly get the keys out of the ignition, I was shaking so much. It was Granny who heard me fumbling with the front door, thank goodness. I didn't want Seraphina to see me in such a state.

'Hello, darling.' Granny pinned a stray wisp of hair into her bun. Her white linen blouse and skirt were as crisp and fresh as usual. So normal that for a second I thought I'd imagined the dark blue car. I glanced over my shoulder. No. It was still there.

'Just in time for lunch. Victoria – what is it? You look dreadful.'

I drew Granny into the sitting room and shut the door in case Seraphina could hear.

'Granny, I'm being followed. Someone followed me all the way from the beach.'

Granny looked at me for a moment. She frowned, then went over to the window.

'Dark blue car? Dark windows?'

I nodded.

'I thought this might happen. It was only a matter of time. They obviously know you're back.' She turned back to the window and stared at the car. Then she waved.

'Granny!'

'How rude.' She sniffed. 'Neither the manners nor the courage to wave back.' She left the window and came over to me. Tipping up my chin with her finger, just as she used to when I was small, she looked into my eyes. 'Don't you worry, my darling Victoria. They won't get the better of us.' She kissed the tip of my nose. 'Anyway, there's nothing interesting for him to see. He'll soon get bored.' She dusted her palms together. 'Now – let's wash our hands. Lunch is ready.'

Chapter Twenty-Nine

Granny had told me that Seraphina's religion had been a kind of life jacket for her in the weeks and months after Maswe's death. But I'm sure that it was Granny's bluff approach that had pulled Seraphina through to dry land. And her no-nonsense attitude to the watching car was just what I needed to calm me down.

For the next day or two, as soon as I got up I looked out of my bedroom window. And the blue car was always there, with the person inside it hunched into a dark shape. Once Granny even tried to take him a cup of tea and a coconut macaroon, but he drove off as soon as she approached.

Then, after about a week, the car was only there now and then, and at no predictable time, and I thought maybe Granny had been right: he'd got bored. I still had that creepy feeling that I was being watched though. Even in Pick 'n Pay I found myself looking over my shoulder, or in mirrored surfaces, trying to catch a glimpse of the person that was shadowing me. Kloete had to be behind this. If he were trying to make me uneasy, it was definitely working.

'Well, Victoria, three weeks until university. Do you good to mix with some young people.' Granny was buttering her toast. She always made sure it went on evenly and right to the edges. 'Better than hanging out with old girls like me and Seraphina. And Hattie.' She reached under the table to pat her. 'Have you got everything you need? Read all the books on the list?'

'Yes, Granny – of course.'

Actually I'd only managed to read one or two, and those only half-heartedly. In fact, half-hearted was exactly how I felt about everything at that moment. Since meeting Abel Nkosana, I'd felt lost and helpless. And I was still haunted by the images of Maswe – if anything, they were becoming even more intense. When they began, I felt trapped and hot and so violently ill I lost all sense of where I was.

'Oh, Victoria,' Granny said, taking a sip of her tea. 'Saw Yvette Obers when I was out walking Hattie. You know she's really rather nice. Said she'd love you to go round.'

I'd seen Miss Obers from my window a couple of times since I'd come back. I felt a bit awkward. I didn't want to be reminded of all that business with the books and the bullying, and I absolutely didn't want to have to go through why we'd left all over again.

'She's offered to give you a hand with the course-work when you start varsity. Not that you'll need it, of course.' Granny brushed some crumbs off the table-cloth into her cupped hand. 'Is that the phone? Won't you get it, darling?'

I ran into the kitchen. There were a few clicks as I picked up the receiver.

'Mom? Dad?' My voice echoed a bit in my own ear. I hadn't spoken to them for almost a week.

'– your grandmother there?' It was only Granny's friend Dorothy.

Granny took the phone, made some arrangement, then put the phone down.

'You know, Victoria, I think I'd better call the tele-phone people in,' Granny said. 'It's been making a funny clicking sound for the past couple of days.' She picked up the receiver again and rattled it. 'Nothing loose. Must be the line.' She looked at her watch. 'I've got to nip down to the shops and to the library before I meet Dorothy for lunch. What are you doing?'

'Oh, I'll stay here and do a bit of reading, Granny.' When she'd mentioned my university course I'd begun to feel a trickle of guilt. Hattie was snuffling about under the table. 'C'mon, Hattie. We've got work to do.' She wagged her tail and hauled herself to her feet. Her claws skittered on the parquet floor as she followed me upstairs.

I took a few books out of the bag they'd been in

since I'd bought them and arranged them on the desk. The idea of the university degree was beginning to lose its sparkle – not that it had really had much to start with. But it was the only way Mom and Dad would agree to my coming back. Before I sat down I opened the Cherry Ames book I kept under my mattress and took out Maswe's letter. It had begun to soften and tear along its creases, so I'd put it into a plastic envelope. I laid it on the desk and rested my hand on it just as I'd done in London every time I'd sat down to do my homework.

It was warm in my bedroom. The sun soaked my head and the surface of the desk. I opened the window. There was no sign of the car today. A breeze kept making the net curtain billow into my face. It was annoying me. I shut the window. It was hard to settle. Victorian poets seemed so irrelevant.

A couple walked past Granny's house. Teenagers – about my age. He laughed at something she said and ruffled her hair. And I felt an ache of loss so strong, I buckled.

When the phone rang it took me a second to work out what it was. As I put the receiver to my ear I heard the clicks again.

'– are you, darling? We're all really missing you.'

'Mom – I'm fine, fine.' What *were* those clicks? There was also a deadness to the sound of the air in the receiver that wasn't normal.

'Dad wants to talk to you. He's got something to tell you.'

Dad came on the line.

'Yeah, Dad. I'm OK . . . Yes – I am preparing for my course. What did you want to tell me?'

And just as he started to talk, I knew. I knew exactly what those clicks meant. It had to be. They were tapping our phone. I had to stop Dad before he revealed anything important, without letting the police, or whoever they were, know that I knew.

'– met a colleague of Ruth –'

I had to stop him.

'Oh, yes, Auntie Ruth. Listen, Dad, I have to go. I'm desperate for the loo. I'll call you back.' I put the phone down.

First followed; then watched; now this. I went back to the window. My hands were trembling as I drew back the curtain to check the street. The car still wasn't there. Not on duty today – at least, not yet.

Dad would know something was wrong. They'd be worried. I'd have to phone from somewhere else. But where? There wasn't a public call box anywhere near Granny's house. Then I remembered what Granny had been saying at breakfast. Miss Obers lived a few houses away. She'd been so earnest about wanting to help me that day in school two years before. Could I trust her? Would I have to explain everything all over again? I didn't know. But she was my best bet.

Miss Obers's was the only unkempt house in the whole street. The hedge, so carefully manicured in front of everyone else's home, was a high, tousled mass. I had to push it apart with my hands to get to the path and front door. The house itself hadn't seen a paintbrush for about thirty years. It was exactly the sort of house that would make people believe a witch lived there. I banged the knocker a couple of times.

'Victoria, my dear.' Her hair had grown since school. It looked a bit like her hedge now. But she was wearing the same upswept glasses, with face powder silting up the frames. She blinked once or twice. 'What an unexpected pleasure!'

I hesitated. I needed to speak to Mom and Dad. But how could I know whether I could trust her?

She smiled. 'Please, do come in, dear. I've been meaning to ask you over for a while.' She swung the door open. The cat on her shoulders leaped off with a screech and darted off into the garden.

'Um, OK. Thank you,' I said. 'I actually came to ask you a favour.'

'Come through, dear.' I shut the door behind me and followed her down a passage. I could smell cats and furniture polish and dust. There were bookcases on both sides of the wall, stacked with books. There were books in piles on the floor too, and of course I ploughed into them, leaving a trail of destruction behind me.

She showed me into a room crowded with sofas and

chairs and paintings and sculptures. There were heaps of books all over the place there too. And I don't know how many cats.

'How can I help you, Victoria?'

'Please may I use your phone? There's something wrong with . . .' I decided to take the plunge – Granny had said she liked her. 'Actually, I think it's being tapped.'

She frowned.

'I know it sounds far-fetched. But please believe me. Well – you know all that stuff about Dad – maybe Granny told you – well, since I came back, they're following me too.' It all came out in a garbled mess. She must've thought I was mad.

'Victoria, of course I believe you. And your grandmother did explain everything to me.' She made an impatient noise. 'I expect nothing less from those brutes. We live in a police state, after all. I'm just upset that you should be going through this.'

She went over to a table and, sweeping a stack of art magazines to one side, pointed to the phone. 'Please, Victoria – it's yours to use whenever and as much as you need. I'll be in the kitchen.'

I dialled Mom and Dad's number. My hands were still shaking.

'Dad – it's me again. I'm calling from Miss Obers's house. She lives two houses away from Granny. I'll give you her number. Dad, from now on, be careful what

207

you say on Granny's line. It's being tapped.' And then it occurred to me that our mail was probably not safe either. 'And I'm sure they're going to read our letters.'

Dad took a sharp breath. 'Mom said there was something wrong. Victoria, tell me truthfully – are you OK? Do you want to come back home?'

Home. I didn't know where home was any more. It took me a few seconds to reply.

'No. I mean, yes, I'm fine. And I want to stay here. You know what Granny's like. She's great.' Dad was quiet on the other end of the line. 'Really, Dad. If I want to go back, I'll tell you straight away and get on the next plane.'

I spoke to Mom for a minute, and then to Charlie, whom I missed so much more than I'd thought possible. I put the phone down gently and stood a while in the middle of Miss Obers's sitting room, waiting for the need to cry to go away.

I heard voices coming from behind a door. I opened it. It led into a big kitchen. Miss Obers was sitting at a table with two black women and a baby. They were all eating. I had to look again. I couldn't believe that I would see black people and white people at the same table in South Africa.

Miss Obers swallowed a lump of food quickly and dabbed her mouth with a napkin. 'Come and sit down, Victoria –' She pointed at an empty chair. There were two keys on the table. 'The big key is for the back gate at the bottom of the garden. Your grandmother has one too, I think.' I nodded. 'And the little one is for the back door. That one, in fact.' She waved her hand at the glass door behind me. 'Victoria –' she looked at me, her eyes bright blue behind her glasses – 'treat my home as your own. Come in whenever you like and use the phone.'

Before I could thank her she began to introduce the women. 'Grace Butshingi lives here. She has the room off this one. Grace was my nanny when I was a child.' Grace nodded slowly. 'Miriam and Samson are her granddaughter and great-grandson. They're staying with me for a while.'

So Grace lived in Miss Obers's house. And her family was staying in the house too. Not even Granny did that. Seraphina lived across the backyard. There was some law about all this, and Miss Obers was deliberately breaking it. If only I'd known what Miss Obers was like. If only I'd confided in her that hot day two years before. She might have been able to do something – I don't know what, but things might have turned out differently.

And then a thought came spinning into my head, tiny at first, then larger and larger until there was no space left for anything else. Maybe Maswe would still be alive now.

Chapter Thirty

Granny was not impressed when I told her about the phone tapping. 'I've got a good mind to complain to . . . to . . .' she began.

But who could we complain to? We were powerless. For a moment, even she was at a loss. Then she straightened her shoulders and lifted her chin. 'We'll not let the bastards win, Victoria.' She gave a chuckle. 'In fact, we'll beat them at their own game. Feed them misinformation.'

I wished I could feel as strong and cheerful as she did. Or seemed to, anyway. I stood in the doorway picking at some flaking paint.

'Victoria, you need to get out for a bit. Take your mind off things. Catch.' She threw me her car keys. 'The cafe at Witriviermond has opened up again. It's really lovely there. Peaceful. You'll feel better. Take Hattie, if you like.'

Witriviermond was about half an hour's drive out of town – part of a nature reserve. Dad used to take me there when I was small. I never could see anything through his binoculars. Except the odd pigeon. But it was a magical place, set in the crook of a mountain; water gushed furiously into a lake, then slid into the river that led eventually to the sea.

The old cafe had closed down when the owner died. Now I saw that it had been cleaned up, rebuilt – sunlight bounced off its glass walls and the metal tables and chairs lined up on the terrace. Hattie tore off as soon as I opened the car door and I ran after her. Granny was right. It was peaceful. And I felt a lot better after we'd belted round the lake.

'Hattie!' I called. 'Let's go and get a drink.' Her tongue was hanging out of the side of her mouth like an old rag. I opened the car to fetch her dog bowl. When I looked round, she'd scampered off and was throwing herself against the side of a metallic-gold, brand-new sports car. Well, not against the side exactly – the car was shaped like a thin wedge of cheese – Hattie's paws were on its roof. She was scrabbling after a bird that had settled there.

'Jeepers, Hattie!' I screamed. 'Get off that car!' I raced over and grabbed her paws before she slid her claws down the car's bodywork. 'Bad dog, Hattie.' She cringed and skulked for a bit near my feet. The car was empty. I looked around. No sign of any irate owner. I checked the paint quickly. Not a scratch, thank goodness.

'Let's go, girl.' I grabbed her by the collar, and made for the cafe.

There was a young woman sitting at one of the tables. She was staring at me and Hattie as we approached. A small paunchy old man pottered up behind her, smoothing his hair down with his palms. He put his arms around her neck and pressed his nose into her ear. Yuck. Rather her than me. She said something to him and pointed at me, and he straightened up. He twitched at his sunglasses. 'Oh no, Hattie – it's got to be the owner of the sports car.' So what? There wasn't any damage to his car.

I could see he was absolutely bristling by the time we reached the terrace. He ripped off his sunglasses.

'Oh . . .' I'd thought there was something familiar about him. 'Good afternoon, Dr Conway.' I knew I'd changed in the two years. Grown taller, for a start. It took him a few seconds to recognize me. And he was completely thrown off course. He opened his beady little eyes so wide his wrinkles opened up and you could see the white lines where the sun hadn't penetrated. He moved his slack mouth around a bit before any sound came out.

'Michael Miller's daughter?'

I loved seeing him so wrong-footed.

'Yes.'

'I heard you'd come back.' He stepped backwards, moved his arms out a bit. He was trying to stop me looking at the woman at the table. Jeepers – he was pathetic.

'Oh, has something happened to Mrs Conway . . . Marguerite?' I asked, my voice sweet and concerned. I leaned sideways to get a better look at the woman he was trying so hard to hide.

'Er . . . *ja*, no, she's fine, fine. At home, making dinner for us right now. For us and . . . our niece, Belinda.' His walnut face darkened and he shuffled his feet. 'Er, visiting us from . . . Potchefstroom.'

Niece, my foot! Who did he think he was fooling?

'Well, good day to you,' he said, and turned his back on me. He sat down at his table. He was trying very hard to behave like an uncle.

I fetched Hattie some water and sat down at one of the tables. I watched that ugly old man. I watched him spooning sugar into his tea and sipping from the cup with his little finger in the air. I watched him laugh at everything the young woman said and rub one of his beige kid-leather pull-on shoes against her twenty-year-old shin – looking up quickly to see if I'd noticed.

It had always been Kloete who was the focus of my hatred; I suppose I'd thought of Dr Conway as his puppet, jiggling about with that stupid leer on his face. But now the more I looked at him, the angrier I became. I felt hot. I pulled my T-shirt away from my neck. I gripped the edge of the table.

The young woman picked up her handbag and

floated off towards the loos. Suddenly I found myself moving towards Dr Conway until I was standing right in front of him.

'How do you live with your conscience, Dr Conway? And you do have some sort of a conscience, because you're not looking very comfortable now that you've been spotted with that poor girl . . .'

He stood up. His face was mangled into a snarl and his breath came out in little puffs. 'What would you know, little Miss Miller?'

'I know what I've seen, Dr Conway. I know you're an evil, smug little bigot. Cheating on your wife is only one of your grubby activities.'

I was quivering. Hattie knew I was upset. She began to growl.

'I don't know what you're talking about,' he hissed. 'Keep your voice down.' People at the other tables were turning round. I knew he especially didn't want his girlfriend to hear.

'You falsify death certificates, don't you, Dr Conway?' I shouted. 'You pretend torture victims die of hunger. Let me ask you this, Dr Conway – how can you make a body that has been punched and pummelled and pistol-whipped and kicked and beaten with a lead-filled hosepipe and kicked some more and turned into a smashed-up bit of pulp look like someone who hasn't been eating?'

My chest was heaving and I was breathing quickly.

I had to steady myself on the table. He opened his mouth.

'No,' I went on, 'don't you interrupt me. You're on to a winner, aren't you, Dr Conway? Sign off all the deaths for the police, do what they want you to, and your fat pension and your fast cars and the diamonds to buy off your wife are all safe.'

'H-how dare you?' He took a step closer to me. 'How dare you talk to me like this?' His now purple face with its bristly nose was close. Too close. He grabbed my arm.

'Don't you touch me.' I wrenched my arm free. Hattie began to bark. 'You're worse than Kloete, Dr Conway. Because you should know better. Call yourself a doctor? You –' I jabbed my finger in the air at him – 'You're an accomplice. An accomplice to murder.'

He lunged to grab my arm again. Hattie snarled at him and bared her teeth. I flung him away and took Hattie by the collar.

'C'mon, girl.'

I strode over to Granny's car. I'd just unlocked the doors when I heard footsteps behind me. I swung round. Dr Conway had squeezed himself between Granny's car and the next one. His girlfriend was hovering a few metres away, looking pale and frightened.

'Now you listen to me, my girl,' he said to me. His voice was high and spiteful. 'You want to be careful how you talk to people. And what you say to them. You never know what they can do.'

'Is that some sort of threat, Dr Conway?' He'd spent too much time with Kloete – he sounded just like him. I gave a dry laugh and opened the driver's door. Hattie clambered in and, as I ducked to follow her, I heard him say, 'Wait and see.'

I slammed the door and turned the key in the ignition. I had to wait for him to shuffle out from between the cars before I could leave. I would have loved to zoom off, but then I wouldn't have seen him go up to Belinda, or whatever her name was, and try to snuggle up to her – only to be shoved away, a look of disgust and horror on her face.

Chapter Thirty-One

The next day Hattie was dead. Poisoned. I found her body strung out in the middle of the back lawn.

I must have screamed, because Seraphina came running. She wrapped me in her arms. Then Granny ran out too, her dressing gown flying behind her, one slipper on. None of us said anything. I knelt down and kissed Hattie's cold nose. She smelled of stale fish. Then Granny and Seraphina helped me back into the house.

Seraphina made me a cup of black tea. I don't know if I drank it. I vaguely heard Granny on the phone, talking to the vet. I couldn't sit there. Not one second longer. I grabbed the telephone directory from the bookshelf. My fingers didn't want to work. Conn, Connor, Conway. Conway, A.; Conway, B.; Conway, Dr C., 52 Manor Drive.

'Vict—' Granny shouted.

I couldn't stop to listen. I snatched the car keys off

the little hall table and ran out of the house. A blind fury was beginning to white out my mind. You bastard, Conway. I'm going to get you. You killed my dog. Fifty-two Manor Drive. I'm going to get you. Over and over, I repeated this mantra, racing down and across streets. I drove round in circles for a while, lost, and it made me boil. Bastard. You bastard, Conway.

Manor Drive – at last. Hushed and green, with English-style mansions behind three-metre-high fences. I parked Granny's car wildly, at an angle to the kerb, and flung open the door. I gulped at the cold morning air for a second. Then tore across the road. Number fifty-two was the corner house. The huge iron gates were locked shut. I tried to shake them open. When nothing happened, I pressed the buzzer on the pillar at the side.

'Open the gates, you coward!' I shouted. I pushed the buzzer again and again. 'I know you're in there. Let me in.'

'Can I help you?' An elderly man had stopped his car in the drive next door. His stare started at my bare feet and travelled past my scruffy jeans and up to my pyjama top and tangled hair. I'd been half dressed when I'd spotted Hattie from the bathroom window.

'I need to speak to Dr Conway.'

'I'm not sure I should be telling you this, but the Conways left for their holiday early this morning.

You'd be wasting your time if you hung around here any longer.' He rolled up his window and drove off.

I gave the gates an extra rattle, then picked my way over the tarmac back to Granny's car. I got in and shut the door. I was shivering. So Conway'd scuttled off. Probably thought he'd get going before I could blurt everything out to Marguerite. Killing Hattie was a warning. I bet he didn't even do it himself, the evil, lying bastard. I switched on the car heater. It made little grunting noises. What now? I rested my head in my hands on the steering wheel. Even if he had been in and I'd confronted him – what good would it have done? None. He would have denied it, I couldn't prove it and he might have got the police to do something else. And it wouldn't bring Hattie back. I started the car and drove off.

All that day, and the next day and the next, I drove, stopping at Granny's only to eat some dinner and to sleep. I drove around the town through suburbs I'd hardly known existed. Through poor-white areas of identical, no-hope, falling-down houses, with discoloured underwear hanging from the windows. Down to the docks, and the smell of salt water and oil and the boom of ships' horns. Past the railways and golf courses and sports fields, and the endless shopping centres that had sprung up all over the place. Sometimes the dark blue car was behind me, sometimes not. I didn't care.

I kept on driving until finally on the third day in the late afternoon I stopped outside our old house. I hadn't been able to bring myself to go back there before. I knew Granny and Seraphina had cleared the house and put stuff into storage. But even so, I suppose I thought I'd still see our lives suspended in mid-action – Charlie as the baby he was then, a small statue on the grass with a frozen falling castle of blocks, or Hattie stuck in the air, trying to catch a bird.

Or Maswe in his blue shirt leaving me. Too far away to call him back, too far away to stop him going.

I parked the car on the verge. Dad had arranged for the house to be rented out to another family. I hoped none of them would appear. I sat there for a while, thinking about our lives in that house. Everything seemed so innocent then.

It was getting late. A girl was coming up the road, pushing a pram. I saw her first in the rear-view mirror. Then she drew level with the car. Her head was down. One of the wheels of the pram squeaked. I felt a rush of all sorts of emotions – a fresh surge of anger, mixed up with bitterness and curiosity. Should I say hello, or should I just let her move on?

'Elise?' I got out of the car.

She looked up. She was back wearing glasses; when she saw me her eyebrows shot up above the level of the frames. And her mouth made a perfect 'O' in the middle of her fat-again face.

'Victoria!' She let go of the handle of the pram to scrape her fingers through her lank hair. For a split second she smiled, then she scowled. 'What the hell are you doing here?' She didn't seem to know how to react.

'I've come back. Staying with my grandmother.' I'd met Elise in my imagination so many times. I'd screamed at her, spoken to her in icy, superior tones, dismissed her. But it was different actually seeing her in the flesh. I found myself talking to her as I used to before Micheline took her over. 'Is that a new –' I looked into the pram. The baby was wearing blue – 'brother?'

A bright red blotch grew out of Elise's neck and began to cover her face. She looked away for a second, then gave the pram a rough joggle. 'No. It's mine.'

'What? Really?'

'And Craig's.'

It did look like a mini Craig. It even had a flaky scalp. I glanced at her left hand.

'No,' Elise said, 'we're not married. Couldn't cope, could he? Ran away to Jo'burg.' A big tear hovered on the rim of one eye, then splashed on to her cheek. 'With Micheline.'

The baby started churning under its blanket, then punching the air. It made a creaking noise.

'Don't you dare start crying,' Elise muttered. She gave the pram another jostle.

Jeepers. I began to feel sorry for her. And she must have realized, because suddenly she turned nasty.

'Anyway – don't you start feeling all superior.' Her mottled face was all snarled up. 'Count your lucky stars my mother didn't get you arrested.' The baby began a full-scale scream. 'Now get out of my way.' Jerking the pram so violently I thought she would flip the baby right out of it, she stormed off.

'Elise – careful!' I shouted at her back.

She stopped. Swung round, dragging the pram back to where I was standing.

'Don't you dare tell me how to behave with my baby, you disgusting Kaffir-lover. No wonder your father had to run away – he couldn't hold his head up with a daughter like you.'

She sounded just like her mother. For the first time in days I smiled. Elise looked confused. She frowned, then turned again and marched off. The baby's hoarse screams faded as the distance between us grew.

Vengefulness towards Elise had burned in me like an acid for two years. Now it had gone. There just wasn't any point in it any more.

I got back in the car. I swept my hands over my face and through my hair. For three days I'd been driving in decreasing circles. I had known where I was heading without admitting it to myself.

Chapter Thirty-Two

The Berg Street police station. All my nightmares came from there and led back there, creeping up behind me and jolting me with searing breath and icy claws. Whereas before the images had moved in a speeding-up but logical line, now they came at me in no particular order, bombarding me, hammering at me from every side – Stompie's kissing noises, the smell of toilets, the out-of-date magazines, sand in my shoes, blood on my shoes – whirling my mind, spinning it until I didn't know which way to turn.

You've got to do this. You must go back. Don't stop, Victoria, I kept muttering to myself. Keep going.

Seeing the police station again – facing it – just had to help. It had to extinguish the ghosts. Nothing else, so far, had been able to.

I drove slowly, creeping down the streets. I was only vaguely aware of hooters pestering me to speed up. Only two blocks to go. One block. My heart coiled into a tight ball and began to pulsate in my throat. I was gasping for air. I swung the car into a side street and braked sharply. The steering wheel slithered under my sweaty palms, but I was shivering. I rested my head on it. I couldn't do it. Not today.

Chapter Thirty-Three

It was a long drive back to Granny's house. I parked the car in the road and just sat there. Seraphina came to get me out. I leaned against her and she gathered me into her so my head rested on her shoulder. I breathed in her warm smell of ironing, camphor cream and the chips she must have been frying specially for me, and I began to cry.

Chapter Thirty-Four

The days passed slowly. The dark blue car was back again, watching and waiting. Sometimes there, sometimes not. I couldn't settle; nowhere felt comfortable. I couldn't read my books. I kept looking for Hattie, kept hearing her claws on the floor. Even Granny held scraps under the table, expecting them to be snaffled up. The house had a stillness that wasn't at all peaceful. In fact, it made me feel edgier, as though I were just on the brink of something.

I think we all felt it. And not just at home. There were more and more gangs of what Granny called 'youths' – young black boys – hanging around. Some near the doors of the Kentucky Fried Chicken and the cafe owned by the old Portuguese couple, but mostly outside the bottle store near the supermarket. And now not just late at night – from early in the morning too. They had a reckless look about them, as though they could do anything they liked, they had nothing to lose.

Often they were drunk, their empty bottles lying where they'd been tossed, and sometimes hurled.

No one parked their cars in that part of the shopping complex. And now the white women on their way from their favourite hairdresser didn't stop to chat in the street, but hurried to their cars, holding their scarves over their new hairdos as though it were about to pour. An air of unease hung over everyone like a storm cloud.

It was Sunday afternoon. Granny and I were reading the papers at the kitchen table when we heard the key scraping in the back-door lock. Seraphina burst in. Something was wrong. She'd said she'd be back on Monday, not Sunday, and she hadn't changed into her work dress and apron as she usually did before coming in. She was still wearing her church-choir uniform; normally crisp and starched, now it was stained and the tabard torn. She was missing her headscarf too, and her now white hair sprang from her head in uneven mounds. She was breathing in short bursts, and I could see that she was limping.

I leaped up from the table, knocking my chair over.

'What's happened, Seraphina? What's wrong?' I picked up my chair and dragged it over to her. She sat down heavily, clutching her bags to her chest. 'Tell me what's happened, Seraphina.' She smelled of smoke and petrol.

'Let her catch her breath, Victoria,' Granny said.

She sat down next to Seraphina, took the bags from her and put them gently on the floor. I noticed they were covered in a powdery grey stuff that looked like ash. There was some in Seraphina's hair and on her shoulders too.

Seraphina turned to Granny. 'Oh, Miss Lydie. Trouble is starting. Big trouble now. We heard of the trouble far away in Soweto. We did not think it would come here to our Location.'

'Shh, Seraphina. Tell us later. Rest now.' Granny put her hands over Seraphina's, which were twisting in her lap.

Seraphina shook her head. 'Maswe . . . He wrote me he wanted change. He wrote me he did not believe in violence. Maswe –'

I'd never heard her say Maswe's name since I'd been back. She'd never mentioned his letter to her. Her voice broke over his name, and she swayed a bit in the chair.

'Young boys – they have been saying for a long, long time, "We do not want to learn Afrikaans." And Maswe, he said that too.'

I remembered Maswe's words: 'Why should we learn the language of those who oppress us?' And I felt a prickle of excitement. Wasn't this just what Maswe had been working for?

'But, Miss Lydie, this is not the same – this is not what Maswe wrote me of.'

Her hands kept moving, her fingers picking over each other.

'Other children are coming into our Location. They are telling our children to leave their schools. Police in vans, they follow the boys.

The children, Miss Lydie, they see the police's guns. They are very, very scared. They believe the police will shoot.'

She squeezed her eyes shut, remembering. 'So the boys they pick up rocks and stones from the ground. And then . . . there is shooting.' Tears began to fall down her cheeks, and she did not even try to wipe them away. 'Police is shooting our children, Miss Lydie.'

The excitement I'd felt only moments before became a stab of horror.

'Not actually at the children, Seraphina? They aren't shooting at the children?' I asked.

Seraphina covered her face with her hands, nodding. 'Children are hurt. I run to help them, but the police they chase me away. I am very, very scared. Young boys smashing and breaking. Burning schools, burning cars . . . everything.' She swayed again on the chair. 'I am running, Miss Lydie. Running away. Miriam – Miss Obers's Miriam – she helped me.'

Granny took Seraphina's hand. 'You're safe now, Seraphina. Let's get you to the sofa so you can lie down.'

Normally Seraphina would have complained about

229

all the fussing, and about sitting on Granny's furniture, and she would have struggled to get up. But this time she didn't. She leaned back and closed her eyes.

Granny took her radio up to her bedroom. She wanted to hear the news, but I didn't. I didn't want to hear the lies, and I didn't want to be reminded of our helplessness.

I took Seraphina's bags to her room. It smelled the same as ever, but now it was bare. The walls were blank and there were no photographs out. Her Bible and hymnbook on the table next to her bed were the only personal objects in the room. If you took those away, there would just be emptiness. It was as though she were getting ready for not existing and I couldn't bear it.

I ran back into the house. She was still lying on the sofa. Granny had spread a blanket over her. She looked so much like Maswe, with her thin face resting against her shoulder. I knelt next to her and felt her breath against my cheek.

Chapter Thirty-Five

There was a tap on the back door a few days later. It was very early, and I was making myself a cup of tea. Miriam, Grace's granddaughter was standing there, shivering in her thin dress. I asked her to come in, but she shook her head.

'No, Miss Victoria. Samson is crying for me.'

'I came round before to say thank to you for helping Seraphina, but you weren't there. Thank you – I don't know how she would have got back if you hadn't helped her.'

She smiled. 'That was nothing.' She stepped closer to me. 'I have a message for you. From Godiva. She says you must go to the soup kitchen.'

'Godiva? When? Did she say why?'

Miriam shook her head. 'That was all she said. Now I must go.'

At first I was irritated with Godiva. Who did she think she was, telling me where I should and shouldn't go? And why the soup kitchen? But then I thought

231

maybe Abel Nkosana wanted to see me. Maybe he'd changed his mind. I heard again the snap of the ice-cream box as he shut it. No. Not likely.

But I kept thinking about her message. And I knew Godiva wouldn't have sent for me unless it was important.

Granny had taken Mom's place on the soup-kitchen rota, and since I'd been back I'd started helping out. I reminded her it was our turn to go that week. But it was Saturday before she finally agreed to go into the Location. She'd kept dithering – which was not like her – constantly pressing her radio to her ear to hear the latest news. The reports said over and over that the uprising had been quelled – they were desperate to reassure their white listeners; they kept stressing the heroism and swift action of the nation's police force.

But it was really only when Miriam told us how bad the food shortage in the Location was that Granny decided finally that we would go – the two of us, because there was no way she'd let me go on my own. She thought her old-lady status would give us some sort of protection. And maybe she was right. But how was I going to distract her if Godiva appeared?

Seraphina cooked a vat of soup and Miriam helped me wedge it in the back of Granny's car. We also filled the boot with boxes of bread, powdered milk and fruit.

'*Hau!*' Seraphina stood with Miriam on the pavement, tight-lipped. 'I wish you would not go.'

'I wouldn't go if I didn't think it would be all right, Seraphina,' Granny said. 'I checked with the police. They've given me a letter to show.'

'Don't worry, Seraphina.' I took her hand. It was as light as paper. 'We'll be back soon.'

Granny showed the permit to one of the policemen lounging at the entrance to the Location. He was young and bored. He flicked his eyes over the letter, chewed down on his gum for a moment, then jerked his head. He didn't care if we went in or not. The sun flashed off the gun slung casually over his shoulder. We were about to move off when the older policeman strode over. He bent to look into the car. His breath stank of stale cigarettes.

'Make open the boot, *ouma*.'

I got out and unlocked it. He rummaged inside. He ripped open a few boxes, the stump of a lit cigarette dangling between his fingers. Some ash dropped on to the fruit.

''S OK,' he said, drawing on the remains of his fag, and flicking it on to the ground. 'You can go. But *pas op* – watch out. This is not a place for people like you.'

I shut the boot and got back in the car.

'Why do they have to carry guns?' I said, after Granny had driven off. 'They make me really nervous.'

233

'You're not the only one,' Granny replied. She coughed and flapped her hand in front of her face. 'So much has been damaged and burned. I'm just wondering what's left of the soup kitchen.'

There were drifts of smoke still hanging over the Location and charred heaps where some of the shanties had been burned. Blackened carcasses of cars too, and a couple of buses stranded in the middle of a field, every window smashed and the sides beaten in. In the distance, fires were still smouldering. When the wind changed direction, it swept the bitter smell of burning rubber, and the stench of sewage and garbage, into our faces. The eeriest thing was the quiet. The only sounds were the repeated rattle and tap of the wind buffeting a scrap of torn metal.

We could now see the soup-kitchen hut. It was scorched, but it looked intact.

'Well, there's quite a bit of the hut left, Granny,' I said as we bounced over the dried-out, rutted track. 'Someone must have put the fire out before it really took hold.'

Granny stopped the car and we got out. I looked around quickly. Would Godiva know I was here? Would she come to the soup kitchen?

A few children came over. They looked at me sideways, holding on to each other, not daring to come too close. I took a few apples out of the boot and held them out. The biggest child moved slowly towards me, then darted forward and grabbed the fruit. She ran off. The others followed her, shouting.

'Come, Victoria. Let's have a look inside,' Granny said.

The door was unlocked. I thought there'd be nothing left. But everything was still there, a bit wet where the fire had been doused.

'Do you think the Primus will work?' I asked.

'Yes, it will. I tried it yesterday.' That low voice. It was Godiva. She was standing in the doorway.

I wouldn't otherwise have recognized her. She'd cropped her hair close to her head and cut her nails off. And she had absolutely not a scrap of make-up on; she looked younger. Vulnerable. Until you looked into her eyes. She was wearing a loose cotton dress with big droopy pockets that not even she could make shapely. It was faded under the arms where the daisy print had been scrubbed and scrubbed.

Granny came over and held out her hand. 'Hello – I'm Lydie Mackeson. This is my granddaughter, Victoria.' Godiva took Granny's hand briefly. There might have been a flicker of humour in her eyes when Granny introduced me. I noticed that she didn't tell Granny her name. 'We've brought some soup for the children,' Granny said.

I went over to the car. Godiva followed me.

'It is good you came today, white girl.'

'Why do you want to see me?' I hissed.

235

'Pretend you do not know me, white girl.' She was as cold and commanding as ever. 'I will tell you. Later.'

OK, I thought, then you can at least do some work. I pointed at the pot of soup. 'We need to take that in.'

We each took a handle of the pot. We carried it into the hut and set it on the Primus stove to heat. She helped Granny and me unload all the other stuff and stack it inside. She didn't speak.

We dragged the trestle table out and set it down on the shady side of the hut. Even there it was really hot. She squatted down in the shadow and fanned herself with a bit of cardboard.

'Look. The children are coming. They are very hungry,' she said.

We dished out soup and hunks of bread and apples and oranges until our arms began to ache. We didn't have time to be watchful.

It was Godiva who first spotted the boys – seven or eight of them, clustered a little way away from the hut. One of them was carrying a bottle of paraffin with a rag stuffed into its neck. The others hung around him, chests out, jostling each other with their shoulders. Their cracked-voiced laughs carried across the burnt-out scrub. Godiva stood for a minute, her eyes screwed up against the sunlight, waiting. When the leader stepped closer, she sprang towards him. Her voice rang out, and with one wave of her hand she dismissed them.

Granny started moving again only when they'd disappeared among the shanties. And that was when I started breathing again too.

When all the food was gone and the last child had meandered off Granny turned to Godiva. 'Couldn't have managed without you,' she said to her, touching her lightly on the arm.

I smiled. She didn't know she was touching a python.

'I've left the powdered milk in the hut,' she went on. 'Perhaps you could tell some of the women it's there. I'll bring some more next time.'

She looked at her watch. 'We'd better go, Victoria. Told Seraphina we'd be back by two.' Granny bent from the waist and straightened. 'Gosh, I'm tired.'

'You sit down in the car, Miss Lydie,' Godiva said. 'I will help your granddaughter put everything away.'

Granny looked like she would protest, but no one argued with Godiva and won. She watched Granny walking towards the car. She began to speak – quietly, but quickly.

'I am going underground. For MK. I do not know how long. I cannot say where.'

I tried to say something. She put her hand up. Scowled.

'You listen to me, white girl.' She folded the legs of

237

the trestle table in on themselves. We carried it back into the hut. 'The police station – in Berg Street – the pipes burst. Big damage. The prisoners have been taken away. Now they are making the jail bigger.' She curled her lip. 'They are building more cells. For more torture.'

Why was she talking about the police station?

We set the table against the wall. She moved closer to me, her tyre sandals scuffing the dirt floor. She took something out of her pocket. Her eyes fixed mine. 'I have thought about you, white girl Victoria. And I have thought about Maswe. I loved him also.' She paused, looked away for a second. Somewhere in the hut a wasp or a fly buzzed. Then she turned back to me, her voice stronger, more urgent. 'MK did not accept you. But you said you want to fight.' She grabbed my arm. I jumped. 'So this is for you.'

She took my hand and closed it around something hard, avocado-shaped.

'What . . . ?' I stared at it. What the hell was it?

There was a glint in her eyes. 'It is a hand grenade, white girl.'

I nearly dropped it. My heart began to chop at my chest. Jeepers. Why was she giving me a grenade? A bomb – for goodness sake!

'MK's next target was the police station. I was supposed to bomb it. But because of what has been happening, MK wants me to leave sooner.' She moved

238

towards the door. 'In fact, someone is waiting for me. I need to go now. So you can do it.' Her eyes glittered. 'If you dare.'

She gave a throaty laugh and strode out of the hut, waving away some flies.

I stood there with that . . . that thing in my hand. I didn't want it. Where could I put it? I set it down on the ground. It was almost humorous – it looked like an exotic egg. But I couldn't leave it there. I picked it up, cradling it in my hands. What if it went off? Could it just go off? How did it work?

I moved very slowly to the door of the hut. My arms were stretched out as far as they would go. With the grenade rocking gently in my cupped palms I scanned the burnt landscape. Godiva had gone. Why hadn't I asked her all those questions? I could feel my heart thumping away at my cotton shirt. Sweat had already begun to plaster my hair to my head.

'Victoria, hurry up! Those youths are coming back,' Granny called from the car. 'We need to move.'

What the hell was I going to do?

Just do something. 'Do something,' I muttered. I took a deep breath. Well, Godiva had had the damn thing in her pocket. So it must be all right to carry around. Just get it home first. Then work something out.

I looked around the hut, my eyes darting from the Primus stove to the easel blackboard to the cardboard boxes we'd carried the food in. I spotted some crumpled wads of tissue paper stuffed into one of the fruit boxes. The apples had been wrapped in them. I grabbed a handful, smoothed them out and gingerly I swaddled the grenade. I made a nest in my bag out of a few more bits of paper, then lowered the parcel into it. I could hear Granny starting the car. She hooted twice. Breathe, Victoria. Act normal. I put my bag over my shoulder. I could feel the swell of the grenade's curved sides knocking against my ribs as I dragged the empty boxes to Granny's car. The gang of boys was moving towards the hut. I slammed the boot shut and leaped into the car.

'About time too,' Granny said. 'Let's get out of here.' She put her foot down. There were beads of perspiration on her forehead. I'd never seen her look so agitated.

I held the bag carefully on my lap. The policemen at the gate waved us down. Oh please, no. Please let them not check my bag.

'Everything all right? All finished for the day, ladies?' Cigarette-breath poked his head through Granny's window. He winked at me.

'All finished,' Granny echoed. She gave one of her stiff smiles.

'See you next time then.' He pulled his head out of the car and rapped on the roof to signal us to go.

As we drove off Granny said, 'Those police – don't

know when they're more scary, when they're friendly or when they're aggressive.' She sighed. 'Jolly glad to get out of there.'

Chapter Thirty-Six

'You all right, darling?' Granny peered at me over the top of her half-moon glasses. We were about to have lunch. 'You're very quiet.'

'I'm . . . okay.' I touched the rough canvas of my bag. I'd hooked it on to the back of my chair. I didn't want to let it out of my sight.

Granny nodded. 'I found the Location disturbing too. Jolly lucky nothing happened there today.' She wove a wisp of her hair back into her bun. 'Not convinced we've seen the end of the trouble yet. Apparently some youths threw stones at some people coming out of the bank this morning, and there was a bit of trouble at the petrol station as well.' She took a sip of water. 'Yvette – Miss Obers – is worried too. She's clearing another room. Miriam and Samson will live with her permanently.'

I couldn't concentrate on what she was saying. I nodded, shook my head, nodded again. I pushed my food from one side of the plate to the other. Panic was beginning to burn a hole in my stomach.

'*Hau!*' Seraphina frowned when she saw I'd hardly eaten anything. I saw the look that passed between her and Granny.

'Have a lie-down, Victoria. Nothing like it to perk one up,' Granny said. 'In fact, I'm going for a nap myself.'

I unhooked my bag and walked up the stairs as evenly as I could. I closed my bedroom door behind me and laid my bag in the centre of my bed. It could have been a cat, curled up in the sun.

Downstairs Seraphina was tidying away the lunch things, clattering cutlery into the dresser drawers. And I knew Granny would be on her bed, her pale pink mohair blanket over her legs, listening to her favourite radio station. I got up and went to the window. Granny's neighbours were unloading their groceries from their car. I could hear them discussing what they would make for dinner.

Everything was carrying on as normal. Except here I was. Alone in my room. With a bomb on my bed. 'Help!' I wanted to scream. 'Help! There's a bomb on my bed!' I put my fists to my temples and shut my eyes.

That night the phone calls began. The shrill ring sliced through the darkness. Mom and Dad and Charlie – something had to be wrong – who else would phone at three in the morning? I was so desperate to answer it I knocked over my glass of water.

'Mom? Is that you? Is everything OK?' Strange. There was no one there. 'Mom? Dad?'

I waited a minute or so. Still nothing. I put the phone down. I got up to fetch a cloth to wipe away the spilled water. On the way back to my bed, I opened my cupboard. There it was. Still there. Still in my bag, draped in the sweaters I'd brought back from London.

I was exhausted. I hadn't slept yet and my eyes were burning. Just as I felt myself dipping into sleep the phone rang again.

'Mom?'

No one there again. I smashed the receiver down.

'Victoria –' Granny tapped on my door – 'I heard the phone. Who was it?'

'No one, Gran. A wrong number.'

I heard her slippers sanding the floor as she pottered back to her bedroom. It was bound to ring again. I lay in wait, rigid in my tangled bedclothes. Just let them try again. I was ready.

At least it took my mind off the grenade for a while.

It didn't ring again. I watched the darkness drain away and early-morning sunshine freckle the floor and the walls of my room. I'd hoped a night's sleep would bring an answer. But I hadn't slept, and I still didn't know what to do with Godiva's bomb.

Fuzzy from lack of sleep, I dragged myself around

all day. I couldn't leave it at home. What if Granny or Seraphina found it? So I took the grenade with me to the library and to the supermarket. I held my bag away from my body – though what the point of that was, I didn't know. If the damn thing went off, six centimetres wouldn't make a bit of difference.

By the end of the day my arm and back were stiff, my stomach was knotted up and I felt so tired I could have fallen asleep on my feet. I hid the bag in the depths of my cupboard again and collapsed into my bed. I must have plummeted into a deep sleep, because the shock of the phone's ring nearly rocketed me out of my bed and on to the floor.

'Hello?' I mumbled into the receiver when I eventually got it the right way up.

No one.

'Who's there?' I asked, irritated now.

Still no one.

More awake now, I shouted down the phone. 'Whoever you are – just stop it!' And I slammed it down.

The phone rang three times more that night, killing any chance of getting back to sleep. And each time there was no one on the other end. Or seemingly no one. Once I thought I could hear breathing. But I didn't stay on the line long enough to find out.

Granny appeared in my room, her long hair silvery against her lilac pyjamas. She sat down on the edge of the bed, rubbing her eyes.

'Not a wrong number then?' she said.

'No,' I said. 'They're attacking from all sides.' Granny knew I meant the police. 'Why don't they leave us – me – alone?'

She sighed. 'We'll simply unplug the phones, Victoria. At night, anyway.'

'But what if Mom and Dad need to get through? What if they need to get hold of us?'

Granny took my hand. 'Darling, we'll tell them to phone Yvette. She won't mind.' She bent to unplug the phone next to my bed. 'I'll go down and disconnect the phone in the kitchen in a minute.'

I sank back on my pillow. Granny billowed my sheet and let it sift down over me.

'Try to sleep, darling.' She went out and I listened to her going down the stairs.

I remembered how safe I'd felt as a small child when Dad came in late at night to tuck me in. Granny was fantastic. And Seraphina. They made me feel loved and cared for. But that tucked-in, secure feeling was different. I hadn't felt like that for a long time now. Tears stung my eyes and I buried my face in my pillow, which suddenly smelled of Granny's lavender soap.

Chapter Thirty-Seven

I rang Mom and Dad from Miss Obers's house the next day.

'Victoria, I want you to come back home.' Mom's voice sounded wavery. 'We're all missing you so much, and I can't bear to think of you on your own with all that happening.' I could hear her swallowing back tears.

'Mom, I'm not on my own,' I said. 'I'm with Granny and Seraphina. And Miss Obers has been really kind too.' I looked at my bag, lying next to the phone. I sounded stronger than I felt.

'When I heard about Hattie —' her voice rose — 'and now there's this.' She broke down, and it nearly set me off too. Dad took the phone from her.

'Victoria, I'll book your flight. Forget about university. You'll come back home. We'll sort something out here.'

'Dad, really, I'm OK. This is home — at least, for the moment.'

He went quiet when I said that. I didn't want to upset them, but I'd fought so hard to come back to South Africa. How could I just give up?

'Dad, please, don't worry about me. Granny thinks they'll get bored soon, and stop all this nonsense. I'd better go – I don't want to run up Miss Obers's phone bill, and she won't take any money from us.'

Miss Obers invited Granny and Seraphina and me over that evening to watch the television she'd just bought. I'd noticed when I was on the phone that she'd made a clearing in her sitting room and arranged chairs in front of the screen.

Seraphina had changed out of her work dress specially. She smoothed down her blouse and skirt for about the tenth time. 'Grace said to me, television, it is just like the bioscope.' She clapped her hands together. 'Is that true, Victoria?'

I smiled. '*Ja*, it's true. Tell me in the morning if you think so too.'

'You're not coming?' Granny looked at me sharply. She was holding a plate of still-warm crunchies to take to Miss Obers. She put it down on the hall table and came over to me. 'Are you not well, darling?' She put the back of her hand across my forehead. 'Seraphina, go without me. I'll stay with Victoria.'

'No, Miss Lydie. I will stay.'

'No.' I raised my voice. 'Neither of you will stay

248

behind. I'm just tired. I'm going to bed soon.' I ushered them out of the door and went upstairs.

I wished I could share their excitement about TV. It wasn't just that the novelty had worn off for me. But my stomach felt as though about a hundred electric eels were writhing and churning about inside it. I felt restless and weepy too, and kind of bleached out with tiredness.

I had a shower and put on my pyjamas. I sat on the floor in front of my cupboard. There was a bulge in the middle of my clothes where I'd stashed my bag. My breathing speeded up. I forced myself to take long, slow breaths. I took the bag out. I lifted the grenade out and peeled off the layers of purple tissue paper very, very slowly. They smelled faintly of apples and made my bedroom look festive. It was like pass-the-parcel – except I was the only one at the party and I didn't want the prize.

The last layer removed, I set the grenade on the floor and lay down to look at it, eye to eye. It did look a bit like an avocado. There was a pin that trapped a kind of lever. Now that I was looking at it closely, I remembered seeing war films where the soldiers pulled out the pin before throwing the grenade. The pin was stuck in place quite firmly. So it's safe then, I said to myself. Safe until the pin's pulled out. It's OK. It's OK.

There were footsteps. Someone coming up the

stairs. Quickly but carefully I put the grenade back in the bag. I just had time to kick all the bits of paper underneath my bed and hang the bag on my chair.

'Can I come in?' It was Granny. 'Just wanted to check you're OK.'

She put her head around the door. 'Good. You're going to bed. Night night, darling. We won't be back late.'

I heard Granny trotting down the stairs and across the hall, the rug muffling her heels for a moment or two. She opened and shut the front door and I heard her tap-tapping down the pavement towards Miss Obers's house. I switched off my light and watched the darkness clot around the objects in the room.

I lay there waiting for sleep. I listened to the rip sound of tyres as cars drove by, scattering bits of tarmac. Their lights wheeled across the ceiling.

I heard Granny and Seraphina coming back, the kettle whistling for Granny's last cup of tea, Seraphina setting the table for breakfast. I was still awake when they went to bed, Granny in the bedroom across the landing, Seraphina to her room across the backyard. My eyes stung around their rims as they drilled through the darkness, staring at nothing.

I got up to go to the loo. My bed felt hot, felt cold, felt hot.

The police station. Kloete. Maswe. The police station. Kloete. Maswe. The police station.

Every time I thought of it my stomach clenched.

Don't close your eyes now. Don't let the images take hold. Quick – think of something happy. Charlie eating ice cream. Hattie – no, not Hattie. Maswe. Back to the police station. Breathe in, breathe out.

I sat up, swung my legs on to the floor. I had to stop this. I had to go to the police station. I had to face it. It was the only way to stamp out the nightmares.

It was four thirty. I pulled on some jeans and a sweater over my pyjamas, dug my feet into some shoes and grabbed my bag.

It was drizzling. The street lights looked like shower heads sprinkling yellow light on to the roads. The car glided on the wet tarmac, the tyres hissing. It made me feel a bit calmer.

This time I didn't stop before I got there. I drew up outside the police station. I pulled up the handbrake and turned off the engine. I forced myself to look at it. It was a bricks-and-mortar version of Kloete. Heavy. Ugly. Menacing. My heart was squeezing.

'Get out, Victoria. You've got to get out. Face it. You'll feel better afterwards,' I muttered.

I took the keys and my bag and got out of the car. I hardly felt the rain. I walked slowly towards the building. Its few windows were boarded up. The front door had been ripped out. It was a dark gash now. They'd begun to put up a rough hoarding. There'd been offices

251

next door. They'd been demolished. The police station stood out from the rubble around it.

I took a few steps closer. Here was where Dad had parked the car. I walked up these steps. My heart began to pound. This was the waiting room.

You see, Victoria – it's all right.

Kloete appeared from there. This was where he led me. Breathe in, breathe out. Down this passage.

There's nothing left, is there? Just a few scraps of old lino on the floor. Sniff, Victoria. Only the cold smell of damp and cement now. Breathe in, breathe out. Down the stairs we went.

No.

I stopped, the wall wet under my hand.

No.

'No!' I shouted. And I shut my eyes.

And then they swarmed at me – every one of my memories of that night – the sand trickling out of my shoe on to the grey lino, the clang of the iron gates, the thick, throat-closing stench of blocked toilets, the flickering green light, the strangely sweet smell of Stompie's uniform, the blood under Kloete's nails.

Every little thing brighter, louder, stronger. Pounding my mind, my ears, my nose.

'No!' I screamed again and again. 'Stop!'

I felt pain, hard and sharp and deep in my stomach. Doubled up, I began to retch. And still the ghosts battered me, hammered and beat and kicked and tore into me. My eyes were open and all I could see was blood and Maswe and blood. I put my arms up across my face and my bag slid towards my shoulder. I felt the grenade bounce against my body.

I don't remember taking it out of my bag. I do remember looking at it sitting cosily in my shaking hand. I remember the comforting feel of its round shape. I remember how I had to pull twice before the pin came out. I remember how my arm swung round in an exhilarating arc as I bowled the grenade into the darkness. And the wide-open, blue sky feeling of freedom as it left my hand.

I heard the explosion just as I reached the car. I turned around. Chunks of plaster and bricks and bits and pieces and coarse dust shot up high into the air. They seemed to hover up there for a long time, strangely silent and beautiful. Then they cascaded down, drumming the ground, joining in with the now heavy rain.

I got into the car and slammed the door. A huge bubble of joy surged through me. It made me laugh out loud.

Chapter Thirty-Eight

10 April 1977

I'd sat up most of the night, but I didn't feel tired. I'd expected to feel anxious or restless. But instead, apart from the occasional fluttery feeling in my stomach, I felt a kind of relief. I'd been waiting for this day for three months.

Three months as a 'banned person'. Banned – what a strange idea. Like smoking is banned, or spitting on the street. Sometimes I felt like a line drawing with two thick black lines crossing out my face. This person is banned. A non-person.

Reporting to the police every day was a nuisance. But never being able to be with more than one person – that was far worse. Not allowed to join in picnics or go out for lunch with anyone. Not even allowed to go to Samson's first birthday party.

And always that feeling of being watched.

I got up from the chair in front of my window. 6.30 a.m. I stretched. Seraphina came up the stairs. I'd heard her unlock the back door really early. She'd been moving round the kitchen for at least an hour.

'Are you awake, my child?'

I went to open the door. She shuffled in, carrying a tray. She set it down on my desk. She glanced at my bed.

'You have not slept, Victoria.' She stood in front of me. There were dark brown half-moons under her eyes and deep creases between her eyebrows and from the wings of her nose to the corners of her mouth.

'And neither have you, Seraphina.'

I put my hands on her shoulders. Her dress stood away from the back of her neck. I'd never spoken to her about Maswe, how I'd loved him, still loved him. And how I loved her. But I always felt she knew. Now I didn't know how long it would be before I would see her again, and I wanted to say something. I tried to speak, but no words were big enough or small enough or soft enough. Seraphina put her long hands to my face, one on either side. She looked into my eyes and she nodded.

Granny tapped on the door.

'Already up, darling?'

Seraphina turned to her. 'She has not been to sleep.' She moved towards the door. 'Come in, Miss Lydie. I will go out.'

'No,' I said. 'Not today. I've had enough of that rubbish. We will all stay in the room together.' I saw

Granny checking to make sure the curtains were closed before she stepped in.

She was dressed for battle. Her hair was coiled into three crisp brioches, held down with a battery of hair-pins. She was wearing her favourite heather-coloured tweed suit, the starched white blouse held to order by a large, shiny brooch. But there was a big, bundled-up handkerchief poking out of her pocket, and her eyelids looked quite pink.

She glanced at the tray.

'Thanks, Seraphina.' She bent to pour the tea. 'Drink, eat, Victoria. You need to keep up your strength.'

I wasn't hungry. It felt too early to be eating. Granny and Seraphina stood side by side, watching me sip my tea and break off pieces of toast. Guardian angels. Was there a slight tremor in Granny's normally very stiff upper lip? I'd put them through so much. Again, I tried to say something. And the only words that tumbled out were, 'I'm sorry . . .'

Granny squared her jaw. 'Twaddle. Nothing to feel sorry about. Don't you forget that.' She gave her jacket a jerk. 'Proud of you.'

Seraphina picked up the tray. Granny followed her out of the room.

'While you're getting dressed, I'll just give Yvette a call. She wants to pop round. Wish you good luck.'

I closed the door. Granny had bought me a skirt and

256

a shirt. They were serious, plain, with no frivolous patterns or frills – but they still made me look young, and a bit vulnerable too. I put them on. I'd refused to have my hair cut. It hung down my back as usual – almost to my waist. I looked in the mirror. Was that the face of a terrorist?

The phone rang. I picked it up.

'Hello,' I said.

There was no response, but I heard someone breathing, a phlegmy catch in the back of the throat.

'You bloody coward.' I said. 'I know it's you.'

Down the line came the kind of cough that starts out dry and ends in a wet smoker's rattle. I would have recognized it anywhere.

'Come on, Kloete.' I hadn't seen him or spoken to him for over two years, but I knew he'd been in my shadow from the minute I stepped off the plane. 'Don't you even have the guts to speak to me?'

'Coward? Did you say coward?' I could tell that I'd annoyed him – he was breathing more quickly and his nose was whistling. 'It was your father who was the coward, *meisie*. But we is happy now. *Ja*, very happy. You betrayed your country and you betrayed your white skin. And now we've got you.'

I felt an almost glacial calm sweep over me. He had begun to sound like a cartoon. 'Is that so, Mr Kloete?'

'Inspector Kloete now.' His voice rose. 'And just because your father runs off to London and he thinks he is so powerful with the big-shot English journalists hanging round the court with their big cameras, that isn't going to make a bit of difference today, *meisie*, when you stand in front of the judge.' He stopped to clear his throat.

Journalists . . . cameras . . . at the court. I felt a jolt of excitement. So Dad had done what he'd said he would.

'You're going down, *meisie*. You're going—'

'*Hou jou bek*, Mr Kloete.' I knew I was being extremely rude. But I didn't care. 'I may end up in prison, but on my way I am going to expose you and all the other murderers like you. Oh yes,' I went on, my voice calm and strong, 'the world is going to find out about your brutality, and the cosy little set-up you have with Cyril Conway. You killed Maswe. I will make sure that he did not die in vain.'

I put the phone down. I slid my feet into my shoes, took a last look around my room and walked down the stairs.

'Granny!' I called. 'Let's go. I'm ready.'

Notes from the Author

We asked Gaby Halberstam to tell us a little bit more about South Africa, the country she lived in until the age of fifteen. Here's what she told us:

1. *Could you tell us a little bit about your childhood in South Africa?*

I was born in the 1960s in a small mining town. I was very young when we moved to Durban, a city on the east coast. My strongest memories of our time there are of the rickshaw drivers lined up along the long road in front of the beach. They were Zulu men with elaborate beaded and horned headdresses. I was mesmerized by the enormous holes they had in their earlobes and the loud war cries they made when they hoisted their rickshaws and made off with their passengers. I remember too the way the sand on the beach was so hot under our feet that it made my brothers and me cry with pain.

We left Durban for Port Elizabeth when I was about seven. PE, as it is known, is a city in the Eastern Cape Province, on the south east coast of South Africa. Compared to Johannesburg and Cape Town, it was a sleepy backwater. The English settlers who'd arrived there in the 1820s had brought with them their elegant architecture and taste for parks, and left a love of English habits – like cricket, and tea at four o'clock. In front of the main library a huge statue of Queen Victoria with her many chins and her grapefruit-like orb stood guard.

My father liked our garden wild. There were perhaps twenty or thirty very tall pine trees that he refused to cut down, and nothing apart from cacti and scruffy shrubs would grow underneath them. It was heaven for my brothers and me and all the other neighbourhood toughies. You could play hide-and-seek and never be found. More dramatically, when the wind came up the pine trees would sway. From time to time, one of them would be ripped out of the soft soil and fall with a high whine. I'd wait inside, half-hoping, half-fearing it would land on our house.

Like Victoria, I walked to and from school. I would walk with two of my three brothers. I too hated the start of a new term and struggled with the scratchy, starchy school shirts. My brothers' shirts were always lovely and soft, having long since been broken in by me. On the other hand, they had to wear my old blazers, with the snot streaks up the sleeves that no amount of cleaning would ever get out.

We had three dogs over the eight years we lived in PE. Hattie is a mixture of two of them: the one, loyal and intelligent and deeply understanding, and the other, always following a smell and getting lost and being brought back to us in all sorts of vehicles, including a taxi. One day, the smell-following dog followed a smell and was never seen again, but we had to say goodbye to the other dog when we left South Africa. I remember deliberately not watching as he bounded off with joy at having a new garden to explore.

The relationship between Victoria and Seraphina is, for me, perhaps the most tender in the book. She is all the nannies we ever loved bundled into one. They were women, often very far from their own children, who washed us, cooked for us, cleaned and tidied after us, watched over us and loved us as their own.

When we left for England I was so excited at the idea of travelling overseas and starting a new life that I hardly gave a thought to what we were leaving behind. With time I began to feel, just as Victoria's father does, a longing for the purple mountains of South Africa.

2. *The population of South Africa is made up of lots of different races of people, isn't it?*

Yes, the fact that South Africa currently has eleven official languages gives you some idea of the diversity of the country's peoples.

In the seventeenth century the Cape – the southernmost tip of Africa – was peopled by the San and Khoi, sometimes referred to as the Bushmen and, insultingly, the Hottentots. Then the Dutch arrived to set up a refreshment station so that they could supply their sailors with fresh food and water. As the colony began to grow, the settlers brought slaves from Malaysia and other parts of the east and Africa. It was the interbreeding of these slaves, the indigenous peoples and the white settlers that formed the distinctive mixed-race group of people known as the coloureds.

Settlers arrived from Germany and France as well as from Holland, and over time these people became known as the Afrikaners.

Control of the Cape kept passing between the Dutch and the British, and the growing number of settlers spread out from the Cape into the rest of the country. There they encountered the indigenous black peoples, like the Zulus in the east and the Xhosa in the centre and south of the country – two

clans of the many that had occupied southern Afı
long before the arrival of the white settlers.

Later, labourers were imported from India to help
cultivate sugar cane, many of whom remained to
establish the large and prosperous Indian community.
In addition, fresh waves of immigrants from all over
Europe kept coming, many of them attracted by the
discovery of diamonds and gold.

With its huge mix of languages and cultures,
South Africa is often called the Rainbow Nation. The
languages spoken by the main characters in *Blue Sky
Freedom* represent only three of the many.

isiXhosa, a language famous for its click sounds, is
spoken by Seraphina, Maswe, Godiva and the other
black people in the book. It is a language of the
Nguni clans, and after Zulu it is the second-largest
language group in South Africa.

Sergeant Kloete's mother tongue is Afrikaans, a
language that grew out of the Dutch spoken by the
early settlers in South Africa. It has evolved into a
separate language, having absorbed elements from
other languages – particularly Malay, Portuguese and
some of the indigenous black languages.

Victoria's family, the Conways, the Westcotts and
Miss Obers are all English speakers. Again, English
was brought into the country by early colonists, and
it too has evolved into a distinctive dialect, with

words and phrases borrowed, stolen and adapted from the other languages spoken in South Africa.

Language in South Africa has been used as a political tool. Maswe was campaigning against the laws passed by the Afrikaans government, particularly those intending to make Afrikaans the language of education in black schools. These laws were yet another attempt at denying black people their own identity and culture, and they helped to spark the 1976 Soweto uprising and the unrest that followed in other parts of the country – including the Location in which Seraphina lived.

I find the languages of South Africa fascinating. I like the way they have become interwoven to form a complex network that ties people together, despite all the violence and attempts at exclusion and separation in South Africa's history.

Afrikaans

bek – the term used to describe an animal's mouth
boeremusiek – literally means farmers' music, but refers to a particular type of music typically including an accordion
braaivleis – barbecue
broekies – knickers
hou jou bek! – shut your mouth!

jirre – exclamation of surprise

Kaffir – a derogatory term for a black person

Kaffirboetie – literally a Kaffir brother, but used in a derogatory way to indicate someone who loves blacks

knobkerrie – a long stick with a knob at the top

koelie – derogatory term for an Indian, or black person

meisie – little girl

'n Bietjie bang – a bit scared

ouma – granny

tackies – canvas shoes, plimsolls

totsiens – goodbye

tsotsi – a wild, perhaps lawless, youth

vetsak – fatty

voetsek! – buzz off! (rude, usually shouted at a dog)

isiXhosa

Ngqundu wako! – your arse!

Wenza ntoni? – what are you doing?

Uyitombi elukhuni emhlophe – she is a stupid white girl

Ufuna ntoni? – what do you want?

3. *Can you explain a bit about what apartheid was and how it came about?*

For decades, when people thought of 'South Africa' they thought of 'apartheid'. Apartheid is an Afrikaans word meaning 'separateness'. It was a system for separating the races, designed to ensure the dominance of people of European descent. It was a system that subjugated the non-white population and reduced them to a state of near slavery.

In the nineteenth century the British passed laws to regulate the movement of blacks. The Afrikaner-led Government later extended these laws, forbidding blacks from moving from tribal areas into areas occupied by whites, and also between districts, without carrying a valid Pass. Blacks were also not allowed on the streets after dark and had to carry a Pass at all times. Without a valid Pass, a person would be arrested, subjected to a summary trial and deported to his or her 'homeland' – an area designated by the government, far from the city, in a part of the country to which that person may never have been. Police vans, like the one in the first chapter of *Blue Sky Freedom*, patrolled the streets, rounding up black people.

Again and again, hundreds of thousands of black Africans were forced off their land and made to live in reserves or designated 'homelands', or made to remake their lives in areas set aside for them by the Government – areas that were usually bleak, with poor housing, little sanitation, plumbing or electricity – very much like the Location that Victoria visits.

It was after the Second World War that apartheid began to gather strength. The largely Afrikaner National Party came to power mainly on the basis of its promises of racial segregation. One of its aims was to protect the poorer Afrikaners from the majority black population, particularly in relation to jobs. There was also a growing sense of nationalism among the Afrikaans population, whose identity was closely linked with its religious beliefs and sense of racial superiority.

4. How else was apartheid enforced?

More laws were passed to entrench apartheid even further. It was decided that there were four main racial groups: White, Black, Indian and Coloured. One of the arbitrary tests for determining race was the comb test: if a comb could not be passed easily through a person's hair, he or she was black. Marriage between people of different races was illegal, and sexual relations between people of different races were a criminal offence. Of course, the relationship between Victoria and Maswe was totally taboo, and against the law, and it is with this in mind

267

that Beulah Westcott reports what she has seen to the police.

Laws were passed providing for separate schools, universities, hospitals, buses, beaches, libraries, parks, public toilets, graveyards, taxis, cinemas and even pedestrian crossings. Of course, facilities for blacks were vastly inferior. Hospitals were badly funded and equipped, education was poor with black children taught only what the Government decided they would need in order to work for a white person. The buses for blacks were crammed with people, run-down and old-fashioned, and a black person was forced to travel third class on trains even if he could afford first or second class. In the parks, I can remember my nanny sitting on the ground because the benches were labelled 'Whites Only'. Without the right to vote, there was little black people could do to change things; they were powerless.

The main opposition parties were the African National Congress (ANC) and the more militant Pan Africanist Congress (PAC). In 1960, spurred on by the PAC, black people collected together in a township called Sharpeville to demonstrate against the Pass laws. Police fired at the unarmed demonstrators, killing and injuring many of them. The Government banned the ANC and the PAC, which were then forced underground, from where they took up armed resistance. Umkhonto we Sizwe,

268

or MK, was the armed wing of the ANC, the group Victoria was hoping to join, and for whom Godiva was working when Victoria met up with her on her return to South Africa.

5. *Maswe is a member of the Black Consciousness Movement – can you tell us a bit about that?*

In the 1970s, led by Steve Biko, a black medical student, the South African Students' Organization began to be more politically active. Biko believed that blacks should reclaim their dignity and fight for their own liberation, and this led to the growth of the Black Consciousness Movement. Maswe was a member of this organization when Victoria sheltered him from the South African Security Police. Maswe was fiercely opposed to the Afrikaans Medium Decree passed in 1974, which made Afrikaans the language of instruction in secondary schools. The outrage young black students felt at being forced to learn in the language of their oppressors led to the uprising in Soweto in June 1976, when armed Soweto police opened fire on unarmed schoolchildren marching in protest. At first the protestors thought the police were firing plastic bullets, but it soon became clear they were not when children began dropping to the ground covered in blood. The death toll was 172 black people killed, and 439 injured.

6. *What did people outside of South Africa think about apartheid?*

Much of the rest of the world watched the events in South Africa in horror. The United Nations Security Council, in particular, passed resolutions with the intention of isolating South Africa from the rest of the world. It introduced an embargo on selling arms to the South African Government and tried to put pressure on companies not to invest in South Africa. South African sports teams were not allowed to take part in international events – particularly painful in a country in which sport is almost a religion.

7. *What was it like growing up in a police state? What does that mean?*

As a child I was fascinated to read about children in England who were happy to ask a policeman for directions. I was terrified of the South African police. I would as readily have confronted a poisonous snake as talk to a policeman.

A police state is one in which the police are used by the state to maintain and enforce political power, often using violence to do so. In South Africa laws were passed giving the police more and more powers – powers that went far beyond just maintaining law and order or solving crimes. Heavily armed, the main

270

focus of the police was maintaining apartheid, and, scarily, they did so without any external control or scrutiny.

The Security Branch was a force that operated even beyond the powers of the normal police. Many believed they were involved in a kind of holy war against the blacks, whom they regarded as savage, stupid and inferior. The security police committed the most brutal atrocities with complete impunity. On the rare occasions that they were challenged, they would lie and cover up the evidence and persuade others under their influence to do the same. Sergeant Kloete is a member of the security police, and Cyril Conway is one of his puppets, falsifying death certificates out of fear for his livelihood and pension, or perhaps because he too believes blacks are subhuman.

8. *Could you tell us a little bit about how you came to write* Blue Sky Freedom?

We left South Africa for England in September 1977, the year after the Soweto uprising. One evening a few weeks later we switched on the television to a BBC news item reporting the death of a young black activist called Steve Biko.

The report mentioned Port Elizabeth, our city, and named a couple of doctors my parents had known. Steve Biko had died in suspicious circumstances while in police custody. Due to the strict monitoring and censoring of information by the South African Government, and the secretiveness of the people involved, we were not aware of any of these events while we were living in South Africa – even though the torture by the police of Biko, and no doubt others, took place not a mile from our house in Port Elizabeth.

Biko's death attracted international attention. At first the Minister for Justice claimed Steve Biko had died of a hunger strike. Later the police claimed he had bumped his head during a scuffle with the police. When the police doctors examined him Biko was naked and chained to a metal grille. They ignored signs of damage to his nervous system, clearly the result of torture by the police. When he lapsed into a coma Biko was driven 750 miles to a prison in another city, still naked and handcuffed, in the back of a Land Rover.

The doctors involved in the Biko case were not alone. Like Cyril Conway, there were many who found it possible to overlook the regular torture of detainees by the police and to comply with police orders that were often at odds with the medical treatment required by their patients.

Reading about Steve Biko, I began to wonder what would have happened if one of the doctors engaged by the police had stood up to them – for example, by refusing to falsify a death certificate. This was the starting point for *Blue Sky Freedom*.

THE TRIBE

Valerie Bloom

The birds should have told us. They should have been silent in the trees, not singing and squabbling as if it was just an ordinary day. The sky should have worn his angry face and the sea should have been boiling with rage. But none of these things happened, so we had no warning. And we were not prepared . . .

Maruka isn't like the other girls in the tribe – she likes to hunt with her bow, deep in the forest. But she wishes she'd stayed in the village the day the Kalinago tribe came and stole her mother.

Two years later giant white sails loom on the horizon and an even deadlier enemy wades ashore. Maruka's tribe welcomes the pale-skinned men but is repaid with treachery. Her world is falling apart, but Maruka won't give up – even if it means turning to her old foe, the Kalinago . . .

Silverhorse

Lene Kaaberbøl

And at that moment the horse turned its head and looked at her.

Horse? No. No horse had such eyes . . . golden, with black slits for pupils. The eyes of a predator that hunts at night.

Kat shuddered, despite herself. Old tales of ghosts and magic stirred inside her, and she felt herself drawn helplessly deeper and deeper into that fierce golden gaze.

From the moment Kat first encounters a silver hellhorse in the rainswept yard of Crowfoot Inn it is her burning ambition to become a bredanari – a keeper of the peace and rider of these magnificent creatures. But Kat's terrible temper, a dangerous secret and a shadowy outlaw all threaten her dream.

THE THING WITH FINN

TOM KELLY

Danny knows he's going somewhere, but he just doesn't know where.

On his way he . . .

- flattens a stuffed otter (with a three-holed brick)
- messes with a dog called The Beast (who bites kids' willies off)
- whizzes on a grey squirrel's home
- feeds biscuits to blue Louie (who puts the 'poo' into poodle).

But however far or fast he goes, Danny can't outrun the memories that are chasing him. Where can he hide when the shadows of his past stretch to forever?

A selected list of titles available from Macmillan Children's Books

The prices shown below are correct at the time of going to press. However, Macmillan Publishers reserves the right to show new retail prices on covers, which may differ from those previously advertised.

Valerie Bloom		
The Tribe	978-1-4050-4782-1	£9.99
Lene Kaaberbøl		
Silverhorse	978-1-4050-9047-6	£10.99
Tom Kelly		
The Thing with Finn	978-1-4050-9021-6	£9.99

All Pan Macmillan titles can be ordered from our website, www.panmacmillan.com, or from your local bookshop and are also available by post from:

Bookpost, PO Box 29, Douglas, Isle of Man IM99 1BQ

Credit cards accepted. For details:
Telephone: 01624 677237
Fax: 01624 670923
Email: bookshop@enterprise.net
www.bookpost.co.uk

Free postage and packing in the United Kingdom